SEEKING REFUGE AND OTHER BIBLE STORIES

LAURA WARE

ACKNOWLEDGMENTS

This collection would not be possible without the instruction and encouragement of the many wonderful Bible teachers I've had over the years. Thank you all for helping me to increase my knowledge and faith.

Once again, Tina Seward stepped up to the plate to copyedit this collection. Any mistakes that remain are entirely my fault.

To Frank and Betty Parker
A couple that have devoted their lives to the study and teaching of God's
Word.
You are an inspiration.

INTRODUCTION

As a Christian and a reader, I love opening up the Bible. It is filled with so many accounts of brave and godly (or not-so-brave and godly) men and women that are not just enlightening and educational but just plain enjoyable to read.

But as a writer, reading the Bible sometimes raises questions. No, I don't try to copyedit the text, but at times my imagination fires up. I want, as Paul Harvey used to say, "the rest of the story."

And because I'm a writer, sometimes I turn to my laptop and try to tell it myself.

While these five stories are based on biblical accounts, I need to emphasize that they are not inspired. They are fictional. Tales that often started with the question, "What about...?" and went from there.

Hopefully you will enjoy seeing these tales and concepts written from another angle. You might even find a deeper understanding of the account it is based on. Whatever you glean from this, I hope it leads you to the original source material.

Turn the page, and get ready to enjoy my fictional take on "the rest of the story."

ABOUT "SEEKING REFUGE"

You will find the laws concerning the Cities of Refuge in Numbers 35:9-29. There is no Biblical record of anyone actually fleeing to a City of Refuge to escape the manslayer. Wondering how that would work caused me to write this story. This is how it might have occurred.

SEEKING REFUGE

Caleb stumbled off the road leading to Hebron and leaned against a large stone, panting. The city shouldn't be far now – it was generally a walk of under three and a half hours from Bethlehem. And he was running for his life – shouldn't he be there by now?

The sun, high in the sky, beat down on Caleb, sweat matting his black curly hair to his scalp. He still carried the axe handle he'd been swinging when...

He shook his head, fighting the bloody image of his friend Micah laying on the ground with the axe head buried in his chest. He couldn't think about that now. He had to get to the city before –

"Caleb!"

Caleb looked behind him. Josiah, Micah's brother, was standing a stone's throw away. Like Caleb, he appeared out of breath, bending over, and resting his hands on his knees. It was hilly in this part of Israel and tiring to traverse quickly.

Alarmed that Josiah had gotten so close, Caleb backed up a couple of steps. "Josiah...I swear, it was an accident..."

"Liar!" Josiah snarled, and started towards him.

Caleb turned and ran, fear giving strength to his wobbly legs. He coughed at the dust that his feet kicked up from the road but fought to keep his pace. Over the next rise...

There! The walled city of Hebron came into view. Caleb saw the open gate, and figures sitting or standing by it. He forced himself to run faster, hearing Josiah's pounding steps behind him.

As he neared the city, Caleb saw men looking in his direction. "Refuge!" he screamed as he approached. "I seek refuge from the manslayer!"

He drew breath to cry out again when strong hands locked around his neck, cutting off his breath. "Now, killer, you die," Josiah whispered in his ear.

Dropping the axe handle, Caleb fought to pry Josiah's hands from his throat. Josiah's response was to squeeze harder, and black stars began to dance in Caleb's vision. He thought he saw people approaching but he feared they would be too late.

Over the roaring in his ears he heard a man's voice: "Release him!"

Caleb fell to his knees and knew he had seconds to live. "Refuge," he wheezed, hoping he could be heard.

Suddenly the hands around his neck were gone. Caleb fell on his side, coughing as he breathed in sweet, wonderful air. He saw several pairs of sandaled feet in front of him. The men from the gate. They had been in time, after all.

Josiah groaned and Caleb rolled around to see his enemy on the ground, a hand on his jaw. A brown-haired man in a dusty green robe stood over him, his hands clenched into fists.

Josiah met his gaze and growled, sitting up.

"Stay down," the brown-haired man instructed.

Josiah glared up at the man. "This fool killed my brother. It is my right to shed his blood."

"I heard him cry out for refuge," the brown-haired man replied. "We all did. You know Hebron is a city of refuge. It is his right to present his case."

Josiah shook his head. "You would force me to leave my brother unavenged?"

"That is up to Jehovah," said a white-haired man who approached, leaning on the arm of a youth. "What are your names? Where are you from?"

"I am Caleb bar-Ammon, of Bethlehem," Caleb answered.

"And I am Josiah bar-Enos, also of Bethlehem," Josiah said, giving Caleb a dark look. "You're lucky I did not have a knife – no one would have saved you from me then."

"Enough," the white-haired man said, raising a hand. "I am Daniel bar-Nathan, one of the elders here. We will listen to you present your causes in the city gate. From there we will determine if we need to send for Samuel."

Caleb slowly got to his feet, watching as Josiah did the same. The brown-haired man took a step to place himself between Caleb and his attacker. Caleb bent down and picked up the axe handle, then followed Daniel who made his way to the gate where other men waited.

۞

Tere were five men who sat in the shadow of the city gate. Daniel sat in the midst of them and appeared to be their leader. Caleb and Josiah stood before them, with the brown-haired man (whom Caleb heard was called Benjamin) standing between them.

Beyond the gate Caleb saw a bustling city. Sandstone buildings lined the main road that led into Hebron. People came and went with no more than a glance at what was happening at the gate. A nearby vendor sold cucumbers and leeks, his wares on a striped blanket that he squatted next to.

Caleb pulled his attention away from the city to the five men who could decide if he lived or died. They were all older, gray- or white-haired, their skin tanned from the sun. One of them snacked on a cake of raisins as he sat, and Caleb remembered it had been a while since he'd eaten.

"Now," Daniel said, looking at Caleb with an unreadable expression. "Give glory to God and speak. What happened?

Caleb swallowed, no longer hungry. "My friend Micah and I went to the forest near Bethlehem to chop wood. My family was enlarging their dwelling, and Micah was helping me cut the wood needed."

"And who is Micah?" Daniel asked.

"He-he was my best friend, like a brother to me," Caleb said. Josiah stirred beside Benjamin but a look from Daniel kept him quiet. "We were laughing, joking, while we worked."

Closing his eyes, Caleb thought about what happened next. "I was trying to chop down a tree – the axe head got stuck in the trunk. I pulled at it with all my strength, and it came free – but the axe head flew off the handle. I didn't know Micah was so close..."

Opening his eyes, Caleb shuddered. "The axe head buried itself in Micah's chest. He died before I could do anything." He turned to Josiah. "I would never harm him on purpose, Josiah – you must know that."

"I know my brother is dead, and by your hand," Josiah spat.

"Did you see what happened, my son?" Daniel asked.

Josiah frowned. "I did not. I was on my way with a message to Micah from our parents when I heard him cry out. I found him on the ground, and this murderer standing over him. I would have killed him then and there, but he fled, like a coward."

Caleb winced. "I knew if I stayed you would have slain me. I had to run."

"I stopped to see if I could aid my brother," Josiah continued. "It was clear that he was murdered. I claim the right of the manslayer, and ask that Caleb be released to me, that I might avenge my brother's blood."

The elders looked at each other. "A moment," Daniel said. The five men huddled in a circle, muttering to each other.

Caleb could feel Josiah's hateful gaze on him. He looked down at the ground, his dirty feet in dusty sandals. Tears burned in his eyes.

He had fled in a panic to Hebron, the nearest City of Refuge. He wished he'd had a chance to go home and explain to his family what had happened – even if he were found blameless, he would be forced to remain in Hebron, unable to go home until the death of the High Priest. Such was the law.

He sensed movement and saw the elders part. Daniel struggled to his feet. "This is what is decided. Benjamin, take a donkey and go to Ramah. Speak to Samuel and tell him what you have heard. If the Lord permits it, perhaps he will come and help us judge this matter."

Benjamin nodded. "I shall leave at once, sir."

"Ramah is half a day's journey by donkey, and it is already afternoon," Daniel said to Caleb and Josiah. "Caleb, you will remain here in Hebron – lodging will be found for you. Josiah, you are welcome to remain here, but no harm must come to Caleb – not until we've heard from Samuel."

Josiah shook his head. "I must go to my father's house, tell them what happened." Brushing a fist over his eyes, he continued, "Caleb will remain here until I return? I will make haste to be back by tomorrow, after I have mourned my brother."

Daniel nodded. "If Caleb leaves before the seer has spoken, his blood is forfeit."

"So be it," Josiah said. He shook a fist at Caleb. "God make me as Micah if I fail to avenge his blood."

"Do not engage in a rash oath, Josiah," Daniel rebuked. "Wait for God to speak."

Josiah took a deep breath. "Yes, sir." Without another word, he turned and stalked out of the city gate, back on the main road.

Daniel motioned to Caleb. "Come, let me lean on you for now.

I will take you to my home, where you may stay tonight. If Samuel rules in your favor, we'll find more permanent housing for you."

Caleb allowed the old man to lean on his arm. "Thank you. I don't know what I would have done if you had not intervened."

"There is nothing to thank me for," Daniel said. "If your words are true, you have nothing to fear. I serve Jehovah. Praise Him."

"Praise Jehovah," Caleb said. Inwardly, he prayed for Micah's family as well as his own.

※

Late the next afternoon, Caleb sat in the city gate with Daniel and the other elders. True to his word, Josiah had returned to Hebron. Caleb noticed that Micah's brother now wore a knife strapped to his belt. He made a point of staying near Daniel, figuring Josiah wouldn't simply murder him in front of witnesses.

People from the city came to the gate and spoke to the elders concerning local business. Caleb found it hard to pay attention to any of it. He settled for squatting in the relative shade the city gate offered, sipping water from the skin Daniel had brought and nibbling on some figs from a nearby bowl.

Looking down the road, he noticed two men on donkeys approaching the gate. He squinted, thinking one of them might be Benjamin but not recognizing his companion.

As they neared, Daniel raised his head. He nodded. "It appears the seer has come with Benjamin."

"Samuel himself?" Caleb breathed. He'd heard of the judge over Israel but had never seen the man himself. He took a good look now.

Samuel was tall and well built. His black hair was long, woven into four braids that swayed as the donkeys approached. Caleb had heard that, like Samson of old, Samuel was a Nazarite, and had never cut his hair.

Benjamin and Samuel came to the gate and dismounted. The elders bowed with their faces to the ground. Caleb and Josiah did the same. Daniel spoke for them all. "You honor us with your presence, Samuel."

As Benjamin led the donkeys through the gate, Samuel spoke. "Given what the young man told me, I knew I had to come. This is of the law, yet it is not often that the right of refuge is invoked."

Caleb stared at Samuel, trying to get a read of what he might be thinking. The man's expression revealed nothing. Would he honor Caleb's request?

Josiah spoke up. "Seer, I am Josiah bar-Enos of Bethlehem. I beg you, sir, do not allow my brother's blood to go unavenged. Grant me the right of manslayer, that I might bring peace to my family."

Samuel's gaze turned to Josiah. "And if he had no hatred in his heart for your brother, but it happened by chance? Do you still want his blood?"

Josiah nodded. "Whether he had hatred in his heart I do not know, but my brother is dead, and that must be atoned for."

"'Must?' Do you declare God's law to be in error?" Samuel persisted.

"I only desire what the law says is mine," Josiah insisted. "Had I reached him before he made his claim, I would have shed his blood, and no one would have judged me wrong."

"But you did not," Samuel said, his rough voice turning gentle. "And regardless of what you want, we must do as God commands. Now, which of you is the man that shed the blood?"

Caleb stood, clutching the water skin. "I am here, sir."

Samuel stared at him a long moment. Then he said, "God spoke to me in a vision last night. He told me you had not meant to kill your friend. That even now, you mourn him as one would for a brother. Is this the truth?"

"I swear by God it is the truth," Caleb said. "I wish I had died instead of Micah. But I didn't mean for the axe head to slip. I ask for refuge, as per the Law of Moses."

Samuel nodded. "And I declare that Hebron shall give you refuge."

"No!" Josiah burst out. "Seer, please!"

"Be silent," Samuel commanded, turning back to Josiah. "You may not harm the man while he remains in the city. If you do, you will be guilty of bloodshed, and your own life will be forfeit."

Josiah's face reddened and he clenched his fists, but he said nothing more. Samuel turned back to Caleb. "You must remain in Hebron, within the city gates, until the death of the High Priest. Should you be found outside of the city before then, your blood will be forfeit. Do you understand?"

"I do," Caleb answered, his heart heavy. He would gain his life, but at a cost. He thought of his family, and tears blurred his vision.

Samuel noticed his tears. "It is the law. We must do as Jehovah has commanded. It is not always easy, but it is right."

"To God be the glory," Daniel murmured. The other elders echoed his words.

Caleb looked at Josiah, who would not return his gaze. "Josiah, I have no right to ask anything of you, but please, will you tell my family what has befallen me?"

"Why should I?" Josiah said. "As you said, you have no right to ask my for anything."

Samuel's eyes narrowed. "Josiah, your grief is fresh, which moves me to regard you with compassion. However, do not let your grief lead you to sin. Bring the news to Caleb's family – it costs you nothing."

Josiah frowned but bowed towards the seer. "As you wish, sir." Straightening up, he said, "I will take my leave now. But I will be watching, Caleb. Don't doubt that."

With those words he strode out of the city, not sparing anyone in the gate a glance. Caleb drew a shuddering breath. He realized at that moment how fearful he'd been of his fate. Part of him had been sure he would die that day.

Daniel spoke. "Seer, I am Daniel, one of the elders here. The day is late. Stay with me tonight and return to Ramah in the morning."

"That is kind of you, Daniel. I shall do so," Samuel responded.

"Thank you, seer," Caleb said, his voice shaky with relief. "I will do as you have commanded."

"See that you do," Samuel said. "As I said to Josiah, God's way is not always easy. But it is always right."

Caleb nodded. He would miss his home. The High Priest was not an old man and was likely to live many years. But he would live, and that had to count for something.

❧

Two years passed. Caleb was given a small house to dwell in and hired himself to a carpenter named Simon. The carpenter sometimes did business in Bethlehem, and he carried letters and money from Caleb to his family, bringing back news and letters that Caleb cherished.

Soon after Samuel had ruled, Caleb's father and mother had come to see him. The trip proved difficult for his father, whose health was poor. But Caleb had welcomed them, letting his mother fall on his neck and weep over his situation.

Though the trip was short, Caleb could see the cost to his father. He urged his parents to go back to his two younger sisters and remain there. He was fine, he lied. No doubt his parents suspected the truth but granted his request.

On this particular day Caleb was using a rough stone to smooth the surface of a wooden table he'd been putting together. The room he worked in smelled of sweat and sawdust. He was alone for the moment, the only sound being the stone being pushed against the wood, getting rid of splinters and creating a pleasant surface that he aimed to make smooth as glass.

The door to the woodshop was open, letting in a slight breeze that didn't quite cool Caleb. He paused in his work, going to the stone pitcher of water Simon's wife had brought in that morning. The well water was still cool in his mouth and he drank his fill.

When he lowered the pitcher, he saw Simon standing in the doorway. Simon was not much older than Caleb's seventeen years, but already had a wife and son. He looked at Caleb, a troubled expression on his face.

Caleb put the pitcher on the ground. "What's wrong?"

Simon had left early that morning to go to Bethlehem before the heat of the day. Caleb hadn't expected him back until closer to evening. Yet it was barely past the midday meal.

The older man sighed. "Caleb, I must speak with you. Come and sit."

Caleb felt a trickle of unease go down his back. He followed Simon outside to a wooden bench that sat next to the door. Sitting down, he said, "What has happened? Please, tell me."

Simon studied his calloused hands. "Caleb, your family begged me to say nothing to you. But I came back as soon as I could because I knew you had to know."

His heart hammering in his chest, Caleb asked, "Know what?"

Simon took a deep breath. "Your father is dying. He took a bad fall off a donkey yesterday, and the physicians believe his end is near."

For a moment, Caleb forgot to breathe. "You...you must be mistaken, Simon. This can't be true."

"He burns with fever – it may be that illness caused his fall. He broke several bones and is simply not strong enough to get well. I am sorry."

Caleb got to his feet. "I must go to him."

"No." Simon also got to his feet. "This is why your family

didn't want you to know. Because you can't go to him, Caleb. You know that you can't."

"I must go," Caleb insisted. "Surely if I explain it to the elders –"

"They will forbid it," Simon said. "They will grieve with you and feel your pain – but they cannot permit it. You know what the law says."

Caleb ground his teeth in frustration. "There must be a way. What of my mother, and my sisters? They need me."

"They have near kinsmen to help them," Simon said, "do they not?"

"Not in Hebron," Caleb said. "It will take time for them to get there – I am closer."

"Caleb," Simon said. "You cannot leave."

"Because you will stop me?" Caleb asked.

Simon shook his head. "Have you forgotten about Josiah? If he hears of your father's illness, he will lie in wait for you. Would you have your mother lose husband and son in one day?"

In truth, Caleb had almost forgotten about his friend's brother. He hadn't seen the man in the two years he'd lived in Hebron. Surely his anger would have cooled by now?

As if reading his thoughts, Simon said, "You cannot count on his losing his desire to kill you. If you leave the city, he can claim the right of the manslayer – and no one will help you."

Caleb felt torn. His father, dying – how could he stay away? Yet Simon was correct, leaving Hebron, even for a good reason, left him at risk.

Looking at Simon, he almost wished he'd kept the news to himself. But how would he have taken *that*? "If you were in my situation, what would you do?"

Simon grimaced. "Exactly what you're thinking of doing."

"Then you'll help me?" Caleb asked. "I need to get out of Hebron without the elders seeing me."

"I shouldn't," Simon sighed. "But I will. Come with me. There is that house we're repairing on the wall. I can let you down with a cord from there."

Caleb nodded. "Thank you, Simon."

Simon said, "I would not be quick to thank me – I may be sending you to your death."

"I will see my father," Caleb answered. "If I perish, I perish."

❈

Simon had been good as his word. He'd lowered Caleb outside the wall, fastening the strong rope to the window so that Caleb could use it to return. With Simon's "God be with you" in his ears, Caleb set his feet towards Bethlehem.

It was late afternoon when he arrived. Men were coming in from the fields, some leading donkeys or oxen. Smells of roasted lamb came from the open door of a wooden home just inside the town. Caleb's mouth watered – he hadn't brought anything to eat, only a skin of water.

He saw some staring at him, but no one approached him to ask questions. He was grateful for that. He saw none of Micah's family among those in the streets – something else to be thankful for.

He came to his father's house, located about a third of the way into the town. It was of yellow stone, with steps outside leading to the flat roof. The door was open, and he saw a couple of women standing in the doorway, no doubt offering comfort to his mother and sisters.

"Caleb."

His heart sinking, Caleb turned to the far corner of the house. Josiah stepped forward, a knife in his hand. "I thought you might think to come," Josiah said, walking towards him, "and here you are. Today my brother is avenged."

Caleb held up a hand. "A moment."

Josiah frowned. "What?"

"My father is dying. You know this," Caleb said. "Please,let him see me with his eyes one last time, and let me comfort my mother and sisters."

Josiah looked uncertain. He shifted his weight from foot to foot. The knife wavered in his hand.

"I only ask for my family's sake," Caleb pressed. "My mother and sisters...they will need help after. Can you ensure they get it? Let me do this and I will put myself in your hands."

"You would entrust me with your family?" Josiah asked. He didn't seem angry – indeed, he appeared confused.

"I know you value family," Caleb said. "Please, swear to me by Jehovah that my family will not know hunger, and let me see my father's face. Then you can do to me as you will."

Josiah stared at the dusty ground. Then looking up, he said, "*You* swear by Jehovah you will not try to escape out of my hand, and I will do as you ask."

"I swear it," Caleb said. He saw the women staring at them. One said, "Do either of you have any regard for the dying? What are you doing?"

"And I swear as well," Josiah said, sticking his knife into his belt. "Come, let's see your father."

The woman who'd rebuked them scowled at them but moved aside to let Caleb and Josiah enter the house. A square wooden table sat in the middle of the room. A small wooden bowl on the table held dates, while a candle battled the dimness in the house.

Caleb heard voices from his parents' room, in the rear of the main room.Josiah paused by the closed door before Caleb could go in. "I will wait here," he told Caleb. "Go see your father."

Nodding, Caleb opened the door and entered the small sleeping area. A bed was against the wall across from the door. A window above it let afternoon light filter in.

Caleb blinked as he saw his two younger sisters kneeling by the bed. They'd gotten bigger in the two years he'd been gone – he wasn't sure he'd recognize them on the street.

His mother was sitting on the bed, holding his father's hand. She turned, and her eyes widened. "Caleb?"

A lump in his throat, he stepped forward. With a cry his mother threw herself in his arms, her blue and white shawl falling from her head. Sobbing, she said, "You should not have come. If Josiah learns of it..."

He hugged his mother, closing his eyes tightly for a moment. "Do not concern yourself with that. Tell me, how is my father?"

Wiping her eyes, she stepped back from Caleb. "The fever burns in him. It will not be long."

Picking up his mother's shawl, he handed it to her. His sisters scrambled to their feet, and he tried to smile at them. But his gaze was drawn to his father.

The older man's body, bathed in sweat, caused the linen tunic he wore to cling to his body. As Caleb watched, a thin foot kicked at the blankets piled at the foot of the bed. His father's breathing was harsh and labored, his eyes shut.

Caleb sat on the side of the bed, taking his father's hot hand in his. As his mother wiped a wet cloth over her husband's face, Caleb said, "I'm here, my father. Your son is here."

His father's eyes creaked open. "Caleb?" he rasped. "Has the High Priest perished?"

Sorrow filled Caleb's heart. While his father's health had been poor, his voice had always been strong. Now, it was labored, as if it were a terrible effort to speak. "No. But I came anyway."

His father's fever-bright eyes didn't leave Caleb's face. "My heart rejoices to see you this last time. But my soul...I fear for you, my son."

"Do not worry about me," Caleb said. "I swear that I will make sure my mother and sisters are cared for. You need not fear for them."

"That...is good," his father said. His voice grew weaker. "Plead with Josiah. Perhaps...perhaps he will have mercy upon you."

"It will be all right, Father," Caleb said, knowing it was a lie, but wanting to comfort his father in these last moments.

"God, be merciful to my family," his father whispered He gazed at Caleb, as if trying to memorize his features. Then, as Caleb watched, his father's face went slack. There was one last, rattling breath, and the hand Caleb held went limp.

❦

After he and his family had wept over his father's body, Caleb left the room. He saw no sign of Josiah, but the two women who'd been waiting now stood in the house. "We grieve with you," the woman who'd spoken to him earlier said, her expression much softer than it had been before.

The other woman nodded, tears streaming down her face. Caleb thanked them and left the house, knowing they would help his mother and sisters prepare the body for burial.

Josiah waited outside near the door, leaning against the wall. He glanced towards the interior of the house. "Your father has died."

Caleb blinked back tears. "Yes," he said. "Please, do not kill me in the doorway of my house. Take me outside Bethlehem and slay me there."

Josiah stared at him, making no move to leave. "My brother's death...it was an accident."

"It was," Caleb agreed.

Josiah looked at the knife in his belt. "I have thought about this," he said. "Do you have a way to return to Hebron after the city gate is closed?"

Caleb stared at his friend's brother. "Yes...but why do you ask this?"

Josiah frowned. "I have no desire to burden your family with yet another death. Go back to Hebron. Tell no one you were here.

I will make sure your father is attended to, and bring your mother and sisters to Hebron, that you might care for them."

Caleb wondered if he were dreaming. "Why would you do this? I killed your brother. You've longed for my death for these past two years."

"Because I believe that if I were the one in your situation, you would extend mercy, though I did not deserve it," Josiah said. "Your family...they showed kindness to mine when you...when Micah died. I will repay that kindness. Go. May God grant you a safe journey."

Caleb took a step towards his friend's brother. "Josiah..."

"I said, go," Josiah snapped. "Before I change my mind."

Without another word Caleb turned and walked away quickly, not quite running.

Praise God, who was merciful, he would live another day. He would be able to care for his mother and sisters.

And perhaps, some day, he and Josiah could be friends.

It would take time. But now, thanks to Josiah, Caleb had the time to use. He would do his best to use it well.

He left Bethlehem without a backwards look.

ABOUT "LET THE CHILDREN COME"

One thing the Bible makes clear about Jesus is that He loved children. He made time for them, and even said that we would have to become like them to enter the Kingdom of Heaven.

I wrote this story from a child's perspective because they were so very important to Him. I wanted to see Him and His death, burial, and resurrection through a child's eyes. Come and look with me.

LET THE CHILDREN COME

Normally, Mary loved the rooftop of her home. From this vantage point she could look at a sea of similar homes and even catch a glimpse of Jerusalem's golden temple. At night she would lie here on her sleeping pallet and gaze at all the stars that sprinkled the sky. She recalled what her father often quoted from a psalm of David: "The heavens declare the glory of God." Looking at the jewels in the sky she found herself in agreement with the ancient king.

But at the moment she was on the roof in the early afternoon, the sun blazing down on her dark hair. She sat with her knees drawn up to her chest and an arm around her beloved ewe lamb, Sasha. While Mary nibbled on a piece of unleavened bread, in the house below her, her parents argued. Even on the roof she could hear their raised voices, along with the cries of her baby brother Eli.

"This is foolishness, Rachel!" her father snapped. Mary could see him in her mind's eye, a short man, bits of clay clinging to his fingers from the potter's wheel. "The man is dead! We must accept it and move on."

"He's *not* dead!" her mother said. Normally the petite woman did not raise her voice to her husband, but now she spoke with fire in her tone. "Peter says he saw him. He's alive!"

"Peter!" Mary's father spit the name out like it was a sour grape. "Peter is an ignorant fisherman who knows nothing! And you've heard the stories...they say Peter and the others stole the body."

"Nathan, you would take the word of a Roman over a Jew?" her mother asked. "Peter wouldn't lie about this...Jesus is alive!"

"Quiet!" Mary's father's voice lowered but Mary still caught his words. "You know what the priests say...we have to be careful. And it matters not what Peter and the others say. Jesus is gone. That is the end of it."

"But Nathan –"

"I said he is gone!" her father snapped. "Speak no more of this."

A moment later the door to the small house slammed. Eli's wails rose and Mary's mother's voice dropped to a low croon. Mary caught a glimpse of her father's curly head as he strode down the narrow street, no doubt to return to his booth in the market where he made and sold pottery.

Mary chewed her bread thoughtfully. She remembered the man they were talking about. It had been a sunny day like this one when she met him, only her family wasn't in the city. They'd traveled to the countryside, to listen to a new rabbi and perhaps speak with him.

Along with many others, her parents listened quietly while the man who called himself Jesus taught them. Mary didn't understand everything he said, but laughed at a funny story he told about having a beam in your eye while trying to get a speck out of someone else's.

The soft grass on the hillside felt wonderful to Mary's bare feet. She was tired from the long day and taking care of Eli while her parents heard Jesus. Her parents wouldn't stop walking though. They made their way through the crowd of chattering people. As they passed by Mary heard things she didn't fully understand, like "Messiah" and "Promised One." She wished she could stop and ask her father about it, but he just kept walking.

They came upon a group of women with young children, a breeze blowing the women's colorful head coverings off their shoulders. In front of them stood a muscular young man with a brown beard who had his arms crossed over his chest and looked annoyed.

Her father went right up to the man and said, "Excuse me. We would like to see the Teacher."

The man rolled his eyes. "You and everyone else. He needs to eat and rest."

"We just want him to bless our babe," her father persisted. "We know he is a holy man. Surely he can spare a moment."

The brown-haired man scowled. "Jesus has better things to do than to deal with your children, Now be off."

"Peter? What are you doing?"

Jesus had walked up while the bearded man was ordering them away. Jesus was of average height, his hair a couple of shades darker than the man he called Peter. Yellow dust stained His blue robe and as Mary watched He stifled a yawn.

Peter turned his back on Mary and the others, his tone half deferential, half paternal. "Master, you should rest. I was just telling these people –"

Jesus shook his head, frowning. "Don't."

Peter's cheeks reddened. "Master?"

"Don't forbid the children to come to me," Jesus said, his tone patient. "The kingdom of Heaven is for such as these," he continued, waving his hand towards the waiting crowd of parents and children.

Mary saw the young man's Adam's apple bob as he swallowed. "Master...I only thought..."

"I understand," Jesus said, laying a hand on Peter's shoulder.

"But this is why I have come." He turned towards Mary and waved her over. "Come here, daughter."

Eli had begun to fuss while the grownups were talking. Mary jiggled him in her arms as she drew closer to Jesus. He sat on his heels so she didn't have to look up at him and laid a calloused hand on Eli's soft hair. The baby's cries died away.

"Teacher," her father said, coming up behind Mary, "please bless our children."

Nodding, Jesus looked at Mary. There were dark circles under his soft brown eyes but He appeared to lay aside his fatigue for the moment. "What is your brother's name?"

"Eli," Mary said.

Jesus grinned at her. "And what is your name?"

She liked his smile, and the fact that he asked her for her name. Most grownups ignored her to coo and fuss over Eli. "Mary."

His smile widened. "That is my mother's name, too. It is a good name. How old are you, Mary?"

"Twelve," she said, trying to stand straighter. She'd just had her birthday and was proud of her age. She knew that before much longer she would be a woman and couldn't wait for that to happen.

As if reading her thoughts, Jesus said, "You will be grown up in due time. Enjoy your childhood while you can, for too soon the burdens of adulthood will be upon you."

Placing a hand on her hair, Jesus bowed his head. Mary caught a whiff of figs on his breath as he spoke. "Father, bless these children, who are precious in Your sight. Help them to love You, as I love You. Amen."

"Amen," Mary echoed, along with her parents. Jesus smiled one last time at her before turning to a young woman leading an unsteady toddler by the hand.

That was not the last time she'd seen Jesus. Her parents would take her to listen to him teach when he came to Jerusalem. And just two weeks ago, when he'd come, her family had joined a throng of people to welcome him to the city. Mary had waved a palm branch bigger than her baby brother and shouted "Hosanna!" with the rest of the crowd. Jesus had passed close by, sitting on a gray donkey, and she'd called out his name. He'd turned and seemed to see her, because He smiled and waved a hand at her.

That had been the last time she saw Jesus. In the days that followed, her father insisted that she stay home with the baby. When she demanded to know why, he wouldn't answer her.

Once she heard her parents talking while she fed Eli some porridge. "Keep them home, Rachel," her father said in a low voice as he stood at the door, ready to head to the market. "Things seem unsettled. The priests are seeking Jesus to arrest Him. It could get ugly."

"But why would they arrest Him?" her mother asked. "He is a good man."

"When did something like that matter to the priests?" her father asked. "Be careful, Rachel. It is better to be silent about Him for now. Anyone following Him…it could be dangerous."

"Mary!" her mother's voice, sounding thick as if she'd been weeping, interrupted her thoughts. "Mary! Where are you?"

Mary sighed. "Coming!" she called back. After stuffing the last of her bread in her mouth, she lay Sasha on her shoulders and began to descend the rough stone steps that marched along the wall of her house.

She was confused. Her father said Jesus was dead, her mother said He was alive. What was the truth? She wanted to believe He was alive. He seemed a good, kind man who didn't deserve to be killed.

By the time her feet touched the ground, Mary came to a decision. Asking her parents would tell her nothing. She would investigate the matter herself. Tomorrow she would set out with one goal in mind: to find out the truth about Jesus.

❦

The sun had not yet risen when Mary quietly rose from her colorful sleeping mat. In the darkness before dawn, she barely made out her parents' sleeping forms not far away on their mats on the roof with her. She couldn't see her baby brother, who slept between mother and father, but she could hear his soft babble in the stillness.

On silent feet she padded to the steps and made her way to the street. Ducking into the dark and quiet home, she found a skin bag she slung over her shoulder. There was a well not far away she could use to fill it with cool water. Next she slipped a brown robe over the ankle-length green tunic she'd slept in.

Plucking a handful of figs from a bowl in the center of a tall wooden table she stepped out of the house –

- and nearly tripped over Sasha, who stood waiting for her by the doorway.

Mary bit back the cry of surprise that leapt to her lips. She glanced up towards the roof, but no one stirred. Glaring at her pet lamb, she willed her heart to slow its rapid beating. "Go away, Sasha," she hissed.

The lamb didn't move. She stared up at Mary with her large eyes, as if she knew what her owner was up to.

Mary shook her head. "You can't come," she whispered. "Stay here."

She'd only taken a few steps when a plaintive bleating stopped her. Turning around, she saw Sasha gazing at her even as her wooly head drooped. The lamb bleated again.

Mary cast another nervous glance towards the roof. If her parents heard..."All right, you can come. Hurry."

The lamb trotted towards her baaing softly. Popping a ripe fig into her mouth, Mary hurried to the well, hoping no one else would stop her on her quest.

Her luck held – the well was deserted. After pouring a little water into a nearby trough for Sasha to drink from Mary filled her water skin. Her heart was pounding as she considered where she was about to go. Her parents would be furious if they knew. They had forbidden her to go near the area.

But her mother had. She said she had, following a bleeding Jesus out of the city to the place that Romans used to execute criminals. The place people in Jerusalem whispered about, calling it, "the place of the skull."

Golgotha. She would start her search there.

☙❧

D awn was breaking and the guards were opening one of the many gates that surrounded the walled city as Mary approached. Her worries that the guards would question her proved groundless; they were too busy dealing with a line of merchants clamoring to enter the city to pay her any attention.

She slipped through the high wooden gate and took a moment to get her bearings. Mary chewed another fig. She'd come out a gate in the northern part of the city. Her destination was ahead and to her left – a small hill that rose up, the rocks forming it arranged by nature so that they formed a likeness to a skull's face.

Mary shivered just looking at it.

Stop, she told herself. *It's just a place. It can't hurt you.* Acting braver than she felt, she walked towards the hill and began the short climb to the top.

Sasha didn't like it. The lamb bleated as it clambered behind Mary and then about midway refused to go further. With a sigh of frustration Mary lifted the trembling animal to her shoulders and continued up to the top of the hill.

All too soon she reached the summit. The place was desolate. Very little grass grew here, the ground tramped down by too many feet over the years. The wind shifted and Mary caught a scent of decay. She remembered that the criminals were often buried in a common grave not far from this place of execution.

Even though she hadn't been here, she remembered that day. It had grown dark at midday, and Mary had lit candles wondering what was going on. Then a few hours later the ground shook, knocking a bowl of grapes from the table, the plump purple fruit spilling onto the floor.

Mary had been frightened. She was alone with Eli, who had been fussy during the darkness and now sent out a wail of fear during the earthquake. Once it was over, she managed to settle the baby. Outside, she'd heard people running in the streets, shouting. She didn't understand what was going on.

When her parents got home, her mother was pale and trembling. Mary's father listened as her mother told of seeing Jesus put to death and shook his head. "You shouldn't have gone there," he told her.

"I had to," her mother insisted. "What will we do now?"

Her father sighed, his shoulders slumping. "I do not know, Rachel. I had such hope..."

Mary was shaken out of her reverie by Sasha squirming on her shoulders. She put the lamb down, almost dropping her as the animal struggled. As soon as her hooves touched the ground Sasha took off, bleating.

"Sasha!" Mary ran after her pet. The lamb raced down the hill and into a nearby garden. Mary went after her, pushing past blooming pink and white roses as she searched.

The lamb was nowhere to be seen. "Sasha!" she called. She heard nothing, not even a baa. Mary began to worry. The garden looked safe, but who knew what might be here?

She searched, her ears pricked for any sounds. A low growl startled her. She turned around, her eyes raking the blooming bushes, but didn't see anything.

The growl sounded again, followed by a bleat. Mary hurried

towards the sounds, worried for her pet. She rounded a corner and stopped dead.

Sasha stood in front of an open tomb, trembling. In front of the lamb were two gray wolves, their red eyes fastened on the little lamb. One of them growled again.

Afraid for her pet, Mary bent down and picked up a jagged stone. "Go away!" she screamed, throwing the stone at the wolves. It struck the closer one in the side and it turned its attention to her with a snarl.

Mary took a shaking step back. She knew better than to turn and flee – the wolves could easily outrun her. The one she'd struck took a couple of steps towards her, growling.

Then it stopped in its tracks, looking past her. The fierce animal lowered its head and tail. It backed away until it reached its companion, who was still focused on Sasha. With a bark it got the other wolf's attention.

The second wolf turned and looked towards Mary. Like the first, it lowered its head and tail. Then the two wolves slunk away, disappearing among the flowers.

Mary ran to Sasha and dropping to her knees embraced the lamb. "Why did you run away? You could have been eaten!"

She heard someone step towards her and she looked up, tightening her grip on her lamb.

A man with dark brown hair stood before her. His robe was white and clean. He crouched down in front of her and smiled. "Are you all right?"

Mary blinked. At once she recognized him. "Jesus?"

He nodded. "Why are you here, Mary?"

It was Jesus, but He seemed different, somehow. The lines of care and fatigue she remembered seeing on His face were gone. His tanned skin shone in the sunlight with a radiance she had never seen on a person before.

"I was looking for you," she said. "My father says you are dead, but my mother says you are alive."

He nodded. "I was dead, but now I live."

Mary frowned. "I don't understand."

"I will explain on the way to your home," he said. Standing, He offered her a hand to help her up.

As Mary reached for His hand, she noticed a terrible scar, as if something at pierced it. She brushed her thumb against the wound. "Does that hurt?"

He smiled again as he pulled her to her feet. "Not anymore."

❈

No one paid any attention to Mary and her companion as they returned to the city. He spoke to her as they walked, and Mary found the things He said to be wonderful, if a little confusing. He patiently answered her questions until they arrived at her home.

As they approached, the door flew open and Mary's father stepped out. When he saw her he let out with a huge sigh. "Mary! Praise God, your mother and I have been worried –"

He saw who was with her and stopped talking, his eyes widening.

Jesus stepped forward. "I have returned your child to you, Nathan," he said gently. "Do you now believe?"

Before her father could reply her mother stepped out, holding Eli in her arms. She saw Jesus standing with Mary and with a cry of joy fell to her knees. "Lord!"

Mary's father knelt as well. "My Lord, forgive my unbelief!"

Jesus laid a hand on the man's trembling shoulder. "Blessed be your wife, for she believed though she hadn't seen. But I forgive you, Nathan. Listen to Peter and the others, for they will have much to tell you."

"I – I will, Lord," her father said. "I swear it!"

"It is enough that you say you will." Jesus turned to Mary, who cradled Sasha in her arms. "I must now leave you."

Mary frowned. "But I don't want You to go."

Kneeling in front of her, Jesus said, "I must go and return to the Father. But I will not leave you bereft. Remember what I've told you and continue to learn, Mary. And one day we will meet again."

Mary blinked back sudden tears. "I don't understand."

Jesus lay a comforting hand on her shoulder. "You will, child." Standing, He turned and walked away.

Mary's father got shakily to his feet. "Jesus is alive. It is a miracle." He helped his wife to her feet. "Rachel, you were right. I was wrong. Forgive me."

Mary's mother kissed her father's cheek. "There is nothing to forgive, Nathan. We have much to be happy over."

Mary turned, but Jesus was nowhere to be seen. She buried her face into Sasha's wool, missing the kind man already.

But she would do as he asked. She would remember his words, and learn more from the others. It seemed there was a lot to discover, and she was determined to understand it all.

And then, if God was willing, she would see Jesus again. She looked forward to it.

ABOUT "A SLAVE'S RETURN"

Onesimus's story is sketched out in the book of Philemon. I wondered about his point of view in this. How did he become a Christian? Did he accept at once that he had to return to his master? What was the apostle Paul's role? This short story attempts to fill in the blanks.

A SLAVE'S RETURN

It had been a long time since Onesimus had set foot in Rome. His memories of the city had faded over the years away and were colored by his experience in the slave market.

He spied one across the street. Men, women, and even a couple of children chained and lined up next to a platform. A fat man with a whip in one hand seemed to be extolling the virtues of a muscular lad who wore chains on his wrists and ankles and nothing else. He glared at the people bidding for him, and Onesimus had no doubt the lad's back was covered with stripes from the whip.

He circled one of his wrists with his fingers, the old marks of the chains he'd worn for so long still visible. He wished he'd thought to wear a long-sleeved tunic, instead of the sleeveless shirt he wore along with trousers.

But his escape from his master had been one of impulse and opportunity. There hadn't been much time for a plan.

So many people! Onesimus was jostled more than once by someone who seemed to be in some kind of hurry. The bright colors of clothing worn by the Romans hurt his tired eyes. Voices seemed to echo off the stone buildings and hurt his ears.

When had he slept last? The trip to Rome from Colossae had been difficult and long. Onesimus had used some of the gold he'd taken from his master to book passage on a ship, but even there he never felt completely safe. What if someone tried to rob him? Or worse, seized him and sold him as a slave again?

He'd vowed he would throw himself off the ship into the deep before he would be a slave again. He prayed to the gods he'd heard of, even the new one his master Philemon and his master's family now worshipped – Jesus.

Finally, he arrived in Rome. Now, he had to figure out his next move. He'd picked the great city as a destination because it would be easy to hide there and far enough away, he doubted Philemon would think to search for him there.

But the size of the city overwhelmed him. He had no idea where to go or what to do. He still had a little gold left, but it would run out soon, and then what?

Onesimus trudged along, wanting to at least get away from the slave market. It sickened him that people could be bought and sold like food or pottery. And he worried in the back of his mind that he could face that fate again if he wasn't careful.

Roman soldiers with their shining armor and red capes stood in front of a building, watching the moving crowd with suspicious eyes. Onesimus wondered what was there that they guarded. A bank? Perhaps.

His stomach growled, reminding him that he hadn't eaten since yesterday. Perhaps he should find a marketplace and get some food. Once his belly was full, he could think about finding a place to sleep.

A couple of young boys ran across his path, laughing and nearly bowling him over. He staggered to keep on his feet, anger surging through him. "Be careful!"

The boys kept running, heedless of his words. Onesimus watched as they swerved to avoid plowing into a young woman with a jar on her head. The woman swore at them as they shot past, her jar teetering on her head. Onesimus hurried over to help her, but another man beat him there. "Are you all right, my lady?" the man asked, not touching her, but clearly ready to render aid.

The man's face was familiar to Onesimus, and he wondered where he'd seen him before. His blonde hair was shot with gray, and he wore patched dark blue robes. Onesimus thought he'd heard the man's voice before, kind and concerned.

Steadying the pot on her head with her hands, the woman said, "I am fine, stranger. Thank you for your concern."

Nodding, the man said, "I wish you well, then, my lady." Turning, he spied Onesimus standing nearby. His eyes narrowed, then widened as he smiled. "You are one of Philemon's servants, are you not? From Colossae?"

Onesimus felt his jaw clench. He was no servant, but a slave. And an escaped one at that. This man knew his master? Should he run from him?

Before he could move the man rested a hand on his shoulder. "You might not remember me. I'm a physician by the name of Luke. My friend Paul knows your master well. Is he here in Rome?"

"No," Onesimus said. "I...I..."

Luke frowned at him, looking him over. "Are you well? Are you on business for Philemon? Did he send you to check on Paul?"

Onesimus found the questions difficult to answer. Of course, he could lie to this physician, tell him he was about his master's business, and had to go and deal with it. It was a plausible story, especially since Luke seemed to think he was a trusted servant instead of a slave.

He opened his mouth to speak the lie – and his stomach grumbled loudly.

Luke laughed. "I think you might be hungry, my friend," he said. "Come. I was headed to the marketplace to get some food for Paul and the rest of us. You can update us on how Philemon is doing."

"That isn't necessary," Onesimus said quickly. "I have some business to deal with." He made to move away but Luke gripped his shoulder more tightly.

"Paul would be disappointed if I did not bring you with me," the physician said. "And I am concerned for you. You are quite pale, and clearly in need of nourishment."

Onesimus felt trapped. It didn't help that a Roman guard walked by, glancing at them as he passed. If he ran, he was sure the guard would pursue him. And after that...he shuddered.

Luke seemed to study him, and Onesimus tried to control his anxiety. Had he noticed the marks on his wrists? "I do not wish to be a bother."

"It is no bother," Luke said, his voice kind. "Please, I believe this meeting is from the Lord. Come with me and speak to Paul."

The Lord? Who was that? Then Onesimus remembered that this Luke had been with another man months ago, when his master and his master's family began to worship a new god. Philemon had told all the slaves about this Jesus, but Onesimus hadn't paid much attention – what use was a god of masters?

Some of the slaves had become followers of this Jesus, but Onesimus refused. He'd fully expected a beating for not doing so, but Philemon had only looked at him sadly. "I pray one day you'll come to believe in Him," he'd said.

It was clear that this Luke would not take "no" for an answer. Maybe if he went with him, he'd get an idea of his next move. "Very well, sir. Let's see your friend Paul."

⚜

Onesimus was surprised and alarmed to see a Roman guarding the door to the house he and Luke approached. Was this a trick of some kind? Had this Luke led him into a trap?

"Good day to you, Felix," Luke said as they paused by the wooden door of the stone building. "Have you eaten yet? I have bread, cheese, and fruit to share." He held up a woven basket he'd purchased at the market.

To Onesimus's amazement, the guard smiled. at Luke. "I have dined, physician. But I'm sure Aurelius would appreciate your offer. Paul has been quite busy with guests and I'm sure they haven't eaten."

"Thank you," Luke said. Pushing open the door, he gestured for Onesimus to enter ahead of him.

Aware of the Roman guard, Onesimus walked into the house expecting to be seized at any moment. But what he saw once he entered shocked him more.

There was a large room with windows that were currently open, bringing a fresh breeze into the area. Several wooden benches were set against the walls. An unlit brazier sat near a wooden table that had several scrolls resting upon it.

But it was the two people who were behind the table that caught the lion's share of Onesimus's attention. One was another Roman soldier who stood, his helmet off his head and on a nearby wooden chair. There was a chain that was looped in his belt. The other end of the chain was secured to the wrists of an older balding man in a simple brown robe. This man sat at the table and appeared to be reading one of the scrolls.

He glanced up from the scroll and his gaze fell on Onesimus. His eyes were dark and piercing and Onesimus felt as if he knew everything about him in that glance. Then the man blinked, and said, "Luke, who have you brought with you?"

Luke went to the table and Onesimus followed. "I ran into him near the market. He's from Philemon's house..." he paused and laughed. "I'm sorry, my friend, I didn't get your name."

"Onesimus," Onesimus muttered. He couldn't take his gaze off the chain.

"Onesimus," the seated man repeated. "I believe I saw you at Philemon's home when I was there. My name is Paul. How is my friend?"

"He is well," Onesimus said. "Or he was when I left him."

Luke glanced around the room. "Where are the others? I've brought food."

Paul shifted some scrolls to make room on the table for Luke's basket. "They will be back soon. Drag a bench over here, and we'll dine together. I would like to get to know Onesimus a bit better."

As Luke went to get a bench, Onesimus said, "I told Luke this wasn't necessary; I have things to do and would rather not impose."

Paul raised an eyebrow even as he moved scrolls to a bag on the floor beside him. "Please, humor me. As you can see, I don't get out to meet people and it's a pleasure to see a familiar face."

Onesimus looked at the chain again and gulped. "Why are you chained, sir?"

Paul gave a rueful smile. "That depends on who you ask. To some of the Jewish leaders, I am a blasphemer. To certain Gentiles, I am a troublemaker. But I simply claim to be a servant of Jesus Christ and only wish to preach His word."

The guard shook his head. "Your preaching causes more trouble for you than it is worth. If you would just stop talking about this Jesus, it would go better for you."

"I can't stop talking about Him, Aurelius," Paul said, his voice gentle. "Surely you have seen that by now." He glanced into the basket. "You must be hungry – listening to me debate others is no doubt taxing."

The guard sat on the bench next to Paul. "You are a kind man, I'll give you that. I wouldn't mind some food."

By this time, Luke had dragged a bench over and retrieved some wooden plates. Onesimus felt he had no choice but to sit next to the physician. He saw the guard eyeing him and struggled to appear unconcerned.

Before Luke handed out the food, Paul prayed to his Lord, thanking Him for the food and for Onesimus's presence. Onesimus noticed the guard didn't bow his head as Luke and Paul did.

Instead, he closed his eyes while Paul prayed. Perhaps the guard prayed to one of his gods?

When the prayer was finished, Luke handed out warm bread, cheese, and grapes and figs. Onesimus discovered despite his discomfort he was starving and began to eat as soon as Luke passed him a plate.

There was no wine, but Luke passed around cups of water which were sufficient to wash down the meal. Paul asked Onesimus about Philemon and Onesimus did his best to answer honestly. "He talks a lot about this Jesus. Some of the slaves have joined him in worshipping Him."

Paul smiled. "But not you?"

Onesimus had taken a mouthful of bread, which suddenly threatened to choke him. He swallowed before he spoke. "I don't understand how this Jesus has anything to offer slaves, if they must remain slaves after following Him."

"There is more than one kind of slavery, Onesimus," Paul said. "Sin is a crueler taskmaster than Philemon, I am sure. Tell me, how long since you ran away?"

Onesimus froze. When he saw the guard's gaze sharpen his fear spiked up. "Sir?"

Paul's smile was sad. "I remember you. You were one of the slaves that tended to us while we were there. Your wrists bear the mark of chains. And you are fearful here. You don't possess the air of one who is free."

"I – I am free," Onesimus protested. "Philemon set me free."

"Then show me your papers," Aurelius said, his hand on his sword hilt. "Surely your master provided you with proof?"

Fear paralyzed Onesimus. What could he say? Did he dare run, or would the guard outside stop him?

Paul said, "Do not be afraid. My Jesus revealed to me that you've run away from your master. But I will not permit you to be sent to a Roman dungeon."

Luke shook his head. "I saw the marks but assumed he'd been

freed. I felt the need to bring him here, Paul. As if I were compelled. Was I wrong?"

"I don't believe so, my friend," Paul said. "I believe this meeting is from God. We must discover what it means – perhaps it is to save a soul."

Aurelius frowned. "Paul, I'm not certain I can ignore a runaway slave. He should be detained, and word sent to his master."

Paul turned to his guard. "Aurelius, I understand your concern. Let it be this way: I will take charge of Onesimus. Should he flee, add that to my crimes."

"Do you wish to be beaten?" Aurelius asked. "Aiding a runaway slave has penalties your friends may not be able to save you from."

"I am willing to take the risk," Paul said. Turning to Onesimus, he said, "You will stay with us? I could use some help. In turn, I will give you food, a place to sleep, and keep the guards from laying hands on you."

Onesimus stared at the strange man. "You would risk your body for me?"

Paul shrugged. "It would not be my first beating."

Onesimus was torn. His common sense told him to flee this place before they sent for his master. Philemon was Paul's friend, and Onesimus was not.

Or was he? The man was willing to put himself at risk for Onesimus's sake – who did that for a stranger? One on the run?

Onesimus was tired. The trip to Rome had taken much from him. A chance to rest and decide his next moves was welcome.

"I will stay for now," he said. "I don't mind hard work. I will help you."

"Then that is settled," Paul said. Several men entered the house, and Paul smiled. "Let me introduce you to the others."

During the next few days Onesimus found himself in a comfortable routine. At night he stayed at Paul's rented house with Luke and a young man named Mark, who told stories about a man he knew called Peter who had actually been with Jesus.

Onesimus found these stories fascinating. A man who could heal with a touch? Who cared for the poor and the needy? This Jesus was more than he'd originally thought, and he listened with great interest.

Paul had only told him and the others that Onesimus was a visitor from Colossae. Onesimus felt as if he'd been put on his honor, and he discovered he didn't want to disappoint this man in chains.

Onesimus brought coals for the brazier and food from the market. He swept the house and helped Mark and the others keep it neat for the frequent visitors Paul welcomed. Many came to hear Paul talk about Jesus, and some of them decided they wanted to join Paul in following Jesus.

Some of the guests were quite rude, appearing to want to trap Paul in his words. Paul usually bore such people with calmness, but twice in Onesimus's presence cut such men off and told them the conversation was over. The second time it happened, one of the men returned after they'd left, apologetic and begging Paul for another chance. Paul sat down with him, and he eventually converted.

The first Sunday Onesimus was in Rome, a number of men and women came to the house. Sitting on the wooden benches, they sang a song about Jesus, prayed, and listened to Paul as he taught them about how to live what he referred to as, "The Christian Way." Afterwards they shared bread together and drank wine – calling it "The Lord's Supper."

Onesimus sat in back with Mark. He didn't understand most of it, even with Mark's whispered explanations. But all he heard aroused his curiosity. What did this all mean?

Once everyone had left and Onesimus brought Paul his noon meal, he decided to ask what was on his heart. "Sir, you say God desires all men to be saved, and loves all of us."

"I do say that," Paul said. "And you do not have to call me 'sir,' Onesimus. I am not your master."

"Paul, then..." Onesimus took a deep breath. "If God loves us all, why does he permit some of us to be slaves?"

He watched for signs of anger, but the imprisoned man only appeared thoughtful. "Sit, Onesimus. I will do my best to answer your question. Share this meal with me as we talk."

Onesimus sat across from Paul and reached for a handful of figs from a wooden bowl. Paul lifted a hand, "Please, let us first give thanks to Him who provided us with this."

Onesimus snatched his hand back, his face burning. He had forgotten Paul's and the others' habit of praying before eating. Luke, who sat next to him, grinned. "Don't feel bad, Onesimus. I was forgetful of this at first as well."

Paul waited for Mark to sit next to him before he prayed. Onesimus noticed that Paul mentioned him in the prayer – that he would be able to understand God's will for him. He found himself touched that Paul would go to his God on Onesimus's behalf.

After the prayer, Paul drank some water from a clay cup. "One thing you must understand, Onesimus, is that all men are slaves. We either serve the one true God or the evil ruler of this world, Satan."

Onesimus frowned as he added some figs to his wooden plate. "But Paul, I don't serve your God or this person you call Satan. I serve – served – Philemon."

"You don't understand," Paul said. "Satan is God's adversary. He desires to lead men away from Him to their destruction. While you may never have affirmed your service to either God or Satan, you serve one or the other. There is no other choice."

"And if you don't serve God," Mark piped up, "then you must

serve Satan."

Onesimus struggled to understand. "Is this of this world? Your friends do not appear to be slaves of anyone. They are free to come and go as they choose."

"Very good, Onesimus," Paul said as he tore some bread off the loaf that sat between them. "Yes, this is regarding the spirit, not the physical. My friends are God's slaves, as am I. You...you have not chosen to follow Him. That means you follow His adversary."

Onesimus had heard Paul discuss the Spirit with others. "But that does not answer my question. God permits men to enslave other men. How can He do that?"

"Slavery is not part of God's plan for His people," Paul said. "Yet for now he permits it, though He calls for masters to no longer be harsh to those who serve them. They are to remember they, too, have a Master in Heaven."

"Why does He permit it?" Onesimus asked. "My Master follows Him — why didn't you demand he free us when he made that choice?"

"I cannot require what God does not," Paul said. "My hope is that in time, Philemon will see the wisdom in this. But think, Onesimus. If I and others were to proclaim that a Christian slave was free, what would happen?"

Onesimus shrugged. "Many slaves would become Christians."

"But why? Out of a desire to serve God? Or simply to be free, with no intention of doing His will?"

It was a fair point. Onesimus knew that had Paul said his freedom was guaranteed on becoming a Christian, he would do so without thinking about the cost.

"Moreover," Paul said, "Rome would oppress our people more, not less. We would be defying their government with such a pronouncement. The kingdom would not grow."

"But you preach other things against Rome," Onesimus

pointed out. "You say their gods are nothing, that their ways are evil."

"And such is true," Paul said. "But none of this compels a man to follow Christ without counting the cost. Indeed, it encourages one to be sober in their decision; that they know what hardships could await them should they become a Christian."

Onesimus sighed. "It is difficult to understand. If I decided to become a follower, how would my life be better? I am in danger now, should I be caught – would that change?"

"Caught?" Mark asked, looking confused.

Felix, Paul's current guard, barked a laugh. "This one is a runaway slave, young Mark. Only our regard of Paul here keeps him from the dungeons."

Mark stared at Paul. "You take a risk allowing him here."

"I am aware of that," Paul said. "Be easy, Mark. He has not broken faith with me. Turning back to Onesimus, he said, "Would you cease being a slave? No. But you would be free – free from sin, and the penalty due from it. Your guilt would be taken away. That is, if you genuinely believed and obeyed."

Onesimus stared at his plate of figs and bread. Did he believe? This Jesus sounded too good to be true.

"There is one thing," Paul said, his voice gentle. "Once you became a Christian, you would have to make right what you did wrong."

Onesimus caught his breath. "I – I would have to go back? I *can't* go back."

"That is not true," Paul said. "There is a way. I am writing a letter to the brethren in Colossae. Tychicus, whom you met the other day, has agreed to deliver it to them. If you choose to, you could return with him, in the Lord."

"But what would happen to me?" Onesimus said. "I did not mention this, Paul, but I took gold from him. I – I could be beaten. Or worse."

Felix frowned. "A runaway *and* a thief? You are fortunate we guards gave our word to Paul."

Paul sighed. "It is unfortunate, but I will deal with it. I will write to Philemon myself and plead your case. And we will ask God to pour out His mercy upon you."

Onesimus shifted in his seat. He'd done his best for this man, who had protected him from Rome. Dare he trust him in this? "I don't know. I don't even think I fully understand this Jesus. You ask me to change – but I don't understand why or how."

Paul smiled. "I tell you what. Let me speak to you of Jesus. Then make up your own mind. I will not force you to become a Christian – this must be a free choice. But shouldn't you know the facts before you make a final decision?"

Glancing at the guard, Onesimus nodded. "I promise nothing. But I will listen."

༄

Several hours later, Onesimus noticed how Paul's hand trembled as he reached for his cup of water. "You are weary."

Paul shrugged. "I am often weary." After taking a drink he put the cup down and asked, "Do you understand so far?"

Nodding, Onesimus said, "I do. You speak in plain language. And I've heard you say some of this before, to others."

"Can you tell me what you know?" Paul asked. He grimaced as Luke pressed two fingers against his neck. "I'm fine, Luke."

The physician shook his head. "You need rest." He gestured to a curtained off alcove on the right side of the room. "Mark and I can take it from here. You shouldn't overwork yourself, Paul."

The chained man glanced at Onesimus. "Please, Luke. He is close."

Onesimus saw the shadows under Paul's eyes and felt guilty. "I want to think on these things, Paul. Please, do as Luke asks."

Paul briefly closed his eyes. "Very well. Felix, I'm going to lie down."

The Roman guard grunted and got to his feet, Paul slowly rose and would have stumbled if Lucius didn't grasp his arm. Together they went to the alcove. When the curtain was moved Onesimus saw the two narrow straw beds that waited for Paul and his guard. The straw was fresh – he'd made sure of that the day before.

He got to his feet. "I'm going for a walk, unless there's something I need to do here," he told the others.

Mark stood as well. "I'll go with you. I need some air."

Onesimus felt a stab of hurt. He liked Mark, who had treated him like he was anyone else. Until now. "You don't trust me."

Mark shrugged. "Would you trust me if you found out I was a runaway?" He held up a hand before Onesimus could answer. "Let's just go. I'm not Paul, but if you have questions, I'll do my best to answer them."

Seeing he had no choice, Onesimus led the way out of the house. It was cooler, and he wrapped the blue cloak that Paul had loaned him around his body. Mark appeared comfortable in the stained white robes he wore.

The two men were silent for a time as they wandered this small part of the great city. They passed out of the residential area of small homes and through the nearby marketplace, where vendors hawked their goods. Roasting meat scented the air, a more pleasing aroma then the stench of unwashed men and women who crowded the streets.

Onesimus did his best to ignore Mark as he thought. He'd always thought Someone had created the world – it was just a step to believe this God of Paul's was the One. Certainly, this God seemed better than the gods and goddesses that filled Rome. He didn't appear capricious or no better than a man.

And this Jesus...the Son of God became a man, lived as a man, and died, so that Onesimus and others could have a relationship with God. And Paul swore that the life under Christ was far better than any other life.

Was it possible? Onesimus had to admit it seemed possible for Paul. He rarely complained, even though he was under house arrest and had a constant guard at his side. He seemed far more content and at peace then many of the crowd that pushed their way past Onesimus, though they were supposedly free.

But was it possible for Onesimus?

He knew he was what Paul and the others would label a sinner – even above and beyond his running away from Philemon. He understood that becoming a Christian was more than a mental agreement that Paul was right – he would have to change his behavior. And Paul had made it clear that part of that change was going home.

The smell of the sea caused him to look up. Onesimus had wandered to the docks, where a number of ships sat at port. Some slaves were unloading cargo from a large ship that had the Twins on its prow. A Grecian ship?

He turned to ask Mark – and Mark wasn't there. They had become separated somehow, and Onesimus was alone.

This is your chance, a voice whispered to him. *You still have a little gold. Buy passage away from here. Or hire yourself to a ship – maybe this Grecian one. Escape!*

Onesimus felt his pouch. Yes, a little bit of gold – enough to get him away from Rome. Away from Paul, Mark, and the others. Philemon might never find him if he fled now.

He froze. What was he thinking? If he fled, the guards would hold Paul accountable. He would be punished. Philemon didn't know how, but beatings had been mentioned.

Not your problem, the voice insisted. *Paul made his choice.*

And Onesimus had his to make.

It was a wrench to turn his back on the ships, but he did it. He took two steps forward and stopped as he heard his name called out.

Looking to his left, he saw Mark ease past a heavy bearded

man and head towards him. Mark was panting. "I lost you. You must have kept walking when I purchased these." He held up a bunch of grapes.

Onesimus nodded. He had a dim memory of Mark stopping at a fruit stall, but he'd been lost in his own thoughts and kept going.

Mark frowned. "You're pale. Is everything all right?"

Was it? Onesimus waited but the whispering voice was gone. He knew where his path led now, for better or worse.

Plucking two grapes from the cluster Mark held, Onesimus said, "Let's go awaken Paul. I have something to tell him."

⚜

Since Paul was under house arrest, he could not baptize Onesimus, though the slave could tell he wanted to. Mark took him to a nearby bathhouse and immersed Onesimus "in the name of the Father, the Son, and the Holy Spirit."

The bathwater was tepid, but Onesimus felt revived by it. When Mark lifted him out of the water and he opened his eyes, he saw several men in the bath giving them strange looks. One of the attendants said, "It's just those crazy Christians. Pay them no mind."

Onesimus laughed and hugged Mark. "Thank you...my friend."

"Not just friend," Mark said, "but brother."

They returned to Paul's house and Onesimus felt lighter in spirit than he could ever remember feeling. All of Paul's friends congratulated him. Tychicus, a burly man with a red beard, had arrived in Onesimus's and Mark's absence, and clapped Onesimus on the shoulder. "This is indeed good news. Paul has told me of your plight."

Remembering his upcoming journey sobered Onesimus. Turning to Paul, he swallowed and said, "When do I leave?"

Paul, back at his table, paused in his writing. "I am finishing the letter to Philemon now. I think, tomorrow? Tychicus, is that possible?"

Tychicus nodded. "If the letter to the Colossians is done, I see no reason why not. I'm looking forward to seeing Colossae. And you, Onesimus, will be glad to see home again."

"I hope so," Onesimus replied. "But I confess I'm still afraid."

"God will not fail you, no matter what happens," Tychicus assured him.

"Our friend is right," Paul said. "The letter to the Colossians is almost done – Mark, I need you to help me finish it. My hand grows weary, and I must complete this letter to Philemon."

"Of course, Paul," Mark said. He shuffled some of the scrolls on the table until he found the one, he was looking for. Sitting on the bench across from Paul, he waited for the prisoner to finish writing before taking the pen and ink bottle from him.

Onesimus listened as Paul dictated greetings and instructions. To his surprise, Paul mentioned him in the letter, referring to him as "our faithful and beloved brother."

He looked at Paul. "Am I faithful and beloved?"

Paul smiled. "You have not broken faith with me, even though I know you were tempted by the docks." He chuckled at Onesimus's look of surprise. "God showed me. You have done well. And, beloved...from the first I saw you I loved you and desired that you walk in the light. You have given me great joy, Onesimus."

Onesimus ducked his head. To think how close he'd come to failure. But the greatest test lay ahead. As Paul continued to dictate to Mark, Onesimus prayed to his God that Philemon would be merciful to him.

The return to Colossae was not like Onesimus's flight from it.

It was still a long and difficult journey. And he couldn't quite banish the fear that dogged him. But Tychicus proved to be a pleasant and knowledgeable companion. They talked a lot, Tychicus answering Onesimus's questions and teaching him still more about Jesus and His expectations. Onesimus found his newborn faith strengthening thanks to his new friend's instruction.

When they finally approached the gates to Philemon's home, Onesimus felt himself dragging his feet. Tychicus noticed and lay a comforting hand on his shoulder. "Be of good cheer. I have a message for Philemon."

The gatekeeper, a young man called Julius, gaped when he saw Onesimus. "You're back? Is this man returning you?"

Tychicus stepped forward. "Onesimus and I need to speak to your master. Can you ask him to come here?"

Julius looked up at Tychicus. "I will escort you to the house and you can speak to him there. But Onesimus..."

"He is in my care," Tychicus insisted. "He goes where I go."

Julius frowned, but apparently decided not to argue. He called one of the boys playing in the field near the gate to run ahead and inform their master of the arrival of a guest and Onesimus. Then, after locking the gate, he escorted them to the large white house Philemon resided in.

Onesimus felt his steps grow heavier as they neared the house. He passed some slaves who were about their chores and felt their stares bored into his back. He heard their whispers and shuddered – he may have just forfeited his life by coming back.

As the climbed the six steps to enter the house, he prayed for courage no matter what. Then they were inside the house, and Julius led them to a room Onesimus was familiar with – Philemon's office.

A fire burned in the large stone fireplace to his right. Colorful tapestries hung on the stone walls, and thick rugs covered the marble floor. A large window behind the oak desk looked out to the fields where slaves took care of the vegetables that grew there.

Philemon sat at the desk, reading something. Onesimus's master had chestnut brown hair that had begun to gray at his temples. He wore a red long-sleeved tunic that Onesimus knew was his favorite.

When Philemon looked up, his gaze pinned Onesimus where he stood. He frowned and turned to Tychicus. "Where did you find him? I will pay you for returning him."

"A moment," Tychicus said. "My name is Tychicus, and I come on behalf of Paul of Tarsus."

Philemon's eyes widened. "Paul? He is in prison, in Rome. Or last I heard."

"That is true," Tychicus said. "He sent me with a message for you, if you are Philemon."

Philemon glanced back at Onesimus. "I am eager to hear it, but what of my slave? He has fled from me and stolen from me, besides. He deserves punishment."

"It is of Onesimus I must speak," Tychicus said. "Paul asked me to tell you that Onesimus has come back of his own accord. And he has a letter for you that explains matters."

"Of his own accord?" Philemon said. "Is this true?"

Swallowing, Onesimus answered, "Yes, master. I have been in Rome with Paul, and he persuaded me to come back."

Philemon stroked his chin a moment, then said to Tychicus, "Let me see this letter."

Tychicus pulled the scroll from a pouch and handed it to Philemon. "May we sit as you read? The journey has been long."

Philemon gestured to two feather stuffed green couches that faced each other in front of the fireplace. "You may sit, Tychicus. I will have someone bring you refreshment."

"You are unkind to Onesimus," Tychicus said. "He is now your brother – would you treat one of God's people so?"

"My brother?" Philemon's brow knit. "He showed no interest previously. Are you certain this is not some trick?"

"Read the letter," Tychicus said. He made no move to sit on the couch but stood near Onesimus.

As Philemon began to unroll the scroll he asked, "You do not sit?"

"Not until my brother does," Tychicus said.

Philemon shot Tychicus a dark look then began to read the letter. Onesimus watched the different expressions that flickered across his master's face as he went through Paul's message. Disbelief, concern, surprise – and one he couldn't quite read.

Onesimus said nothing, though his feet hurt, and he was tired. He longed to sit but would not do so unless given leave by Philemon. He glanced at Tychicus, who stood with his hands clasped in front of him as if he had all day to just stand there and wait.

Finally, Philemon sighed. He turned and placed the scroll on his desk. Turning back, he said, "Oh, please, both of you sit. I'll be right back." He strode from the room.

Onesimus nearly fell onto the couch. Tychicus gave a groan of relief as he joined him. "I wonder if this is a good thing?"

"We'll see," Tychicus said. "Paul can be very persuasive."

Moments later Philemon returned with a female slave bearing a silver tray of bread, cheese, and a flask of wine. Philemon had her set it on a rectangular cedar table that stood between the couches and then dismissed her. She bowed and left, not without one last glance at Onesimus.

Philemon sat across from the others and poured three wooden cups of wine. "Paul pleads your case eloquently, Onesimus."

Onesimus took the cup from his master and realized he was trembling. He tried to control it as he answered, "That was kind of him, Master."

Philemon sipped his wine. "You are fearful. You should be. I could have you put to death. Or beaten severely."

Onesimus felt his heart sink. "Yes, Master."

"You could do those things," Tychicus said, helping himself to a piece of hard yellow cheese. "But for what purpose? He returned to you freely. I can testify that he served Paul faithfully while he was in Rome. He has changed, Philemon."

"So Paul said," Philemon admitted, taking a piece of bread and dipping it into his wine. He ate it and said, "Paul has also said he will pay me back what Onesimus stole."

"He did?" Onesimus couldn't help blurting out.

Philemon raised his eyebrows. "You didn't know."

Onesimus shook his head. "That is good of him. He pledged my good behavior to the Roman guards. He is a kind man."

"Yes, he is," Philemon said. "He asks me to let you return to him, so that you can continue to serve him."

Onesimus felt a spark of hope. "Is that possible?"

With a sigh, Philemon said, "Here is my dilemma. You ran away and took what was mine. Shall I reward such behavior? What will the others think?"

Tychicus spoke up. "You can forgive him, as you have been forgiven. He has come to try and make things right. That surely should count for something."

"It does," Philemon admitted. "Paul asks much of me, but he has given much in return. There must be some way to work this to satisfy all."

An idea occurred to Onesimus. "Master, I beg you to spare my life. But I will submit to a beating if I must. What I did was wrong. I should not have run away or stolen from you."

Tychicus eyes widened. "You would do that? Onesimus, it could cripple you. Or kill you."

Philemon looked surprised as well. "You offer this? In exchange for your life?"

Fear threatened to choke Onesimus, but he nodded.

Philemon looked into his cup of wine, as if the answers were there. Shaking his head, he looked up at Onesimus. "I thank you – your willingness and confession prove you have indeed been converted. But I will not send Paul a damaged servant. Tomorrow we will go to the magistrate, and I will free you, so that you may return and serve the one who has done much for both of us."

Onesimus couldn't believe his ears. Freedom? He hadn't even considered that. "Master, I thank you."

Shaking his head, Philemon said, "Call me master no longer, my brother. You and Paul have given me much to think about. And you," he continued, turning to Tychicus, "tell me more of how Paul is doing. We here in Colossae have continued to pray for him."

As the other two men talked, Onesimus gazed into the fire. God had provided, as Paul said he would. Tomorrow he'd be a free man, and he already knew what he'd use that freedom for.

He'd go back to Rome and help Paul out as long as he needed him. Perhaps there were other slaves who needed the gospel message that he could talk to. And he knew Paul could teach him so much more than he knew now.

For the moment, he closed his eyes and thanked God that he was His slave – but finally, a free man.

ABOUT "HE WHO HONORS ME"

The story of Daniel is a story of faith tested. My short story expands on Daniel chapter one, looking more into how Daniel and his friends coped with being taken captive to Babylon.

If you want to read further about Daniel, I have written a longer story that you can obtain at https://www.faithjourneys.app/. Check it out for tales of other Bible characters as well.

HE WHO HONORS ME

As Daniel raced through the dusty Jerusalem streets, pushing past panicked fellow citizens, one thought kept running through his mind: *This can't be happening!*

To his right the walls of Solomon's Temple gleamed as the sun's western rays shone on them. Daniel stopped his headlong run a moment, wondering if he should head there. Maybe the priests had word from Jehovah, that He would put a stop to this!

A woman, clutching a baby in her arms, stumbled past him. Daniel reached out a hand to steady her. She jumped back, startled, then relaxed when she saw he was an Israelite. "Is it true?" she gasped. "Have the Babylonians entered the city?"

Daniel spread his hands. "That's what I've heard." He had been at home, enjoying a lunch of lamb stew and warm bread, when his friend Mishael rushed into the house with word that the Babylonians had entered the city and were even now spreading through it.

Daniel's thoughts had gone to his father, a friend and advisor of King Jehoiakim. Ignoring his mother's protests that he should remain home, Daniel had set off for the palace, where he knew his father would be.

The baby in the woman's arms began to wail. She cuddled the child, her own tears falling fast. "The prophets said God would protect us," she murmured. "Just as He had in the past."

"Not all of them," Daniel said, thinking out loud. "There was one – Jeremiah." He felt his apprehension grow as he recalled the strange prophet's words. "He said we would fall, because of our sin."

"But we're God's people!" the woman protested. "What is one prophet among many who say differently?"

"Daniel!"

Daniel turned at the sound of his name. Mishael hurried towards him, his normally jovial face pale, his linen tunic streaked with dirt. "Why are you stopping? I thought you were going to the palace."

Daniel turned towards the temple. Gesturing in its direction, he said, "I thought the priests might have word."

"No," Mishael shook his shaggy dark head. "I saw Azariah – he's been to the temple. The Babylonians are there – they're looting it!"

Gasping, Daniel said, "We have to stop them!"

"Don't be a fool," his friend chided. "One of the priests tried – Azariah said they ran him through."

With a moan of fear the woman Daniel had been talking to fled. Feeling helpless, Daniel said, "We should go to the palace. The king...our fathers...they will know what to do."

"I pray you're right," Mishael said. The two young men began to run towards the palace, fighting their way through a growing crowd. The stink of sweat and fear clogged Daniel's nostrils. He stumbled, falling on his hands and knees and barely avoided being trampled by a merchant pushing a cart of jingling necklaces in front of him. The older man scowled and aimed a kick at Daniel as he swerved to avoid him.

Mishael pulled him to his feet. "Come on. Azariah and Hana-niah were going to the palace as well."

Daniel nodded. The red-headed twins, along with Mishael, were Daniel's closest friends. He prayed they were safe in this madness.

Daniel and Mishael finally came in sight of the palace. Built many years ago, the stone building stood flanked by cedars that were supposed to have been planted by King Solomon himself. Daniel was familiar with the interior of the palace, having come often with his father. He could close his eyes and recall the spacious rooms, their wooden floors covered in thick Persian rugs. He could taste the sweetbreads he and his friends would beg from the cook in the hot kitchen.

To his dismay, soldiers in bright bronze armor surrounded it. One of the soldiers spotted them. "Stop!" he commanded in heavily accented Aramaic.

Heart pounding in his chest, Daniel struggled to catch his breath as he came to a halt. He could hear Mishael wheezing a bit next to him – his friend was not used to running. Bending forward and resting his hands on his knees, he prayed to Jehovah that he would not be killed.

Three soldiers came to stand in front of them. One wore a short yellow cape over his armor; it was he who bid them to stop. He examined them silently for a moment. Then he said, "You don't look like commoners. Who are your fathers?"

Trying to keep his voice from trembling, Daniel said, "My father is Eleazar." He straightened up and met the soldier's gaze. Unlike Hebrew men of his age, this man was clean-shaven. "I am his son Daniel."

"Eleazar..." the caped soldier glanced at a piece of parchment in his hand. "A friend of the king's. And you?" he asked, turning to Mishael.

As Mishael answered, Daniel could not hold himself back. "Please sir, are our fathers all right?"

"Your fathers are prisoners of Nebuchadnezzar. As are you." The soldier gestured to his companions and they stepped forward to grip both Daniel and his companion by the arms. "But rumor has it the king has plans for you younger ones. Be of good cheer – you are going to Babylon!"

Daniel felt his knees weaken. *Babylon?* And what did the soldier mean by "plans?" Before he could ask for clarification the soldier holding his arm pulled him roughly and forced Daniel to walk with him to the palace, to meet whatever fate awaited him.

Jehovah, he prayed desperately as they approached the two large cedar doors that stood at the entrance to the palace. One of them hung oddly, clearly broken by some outside force. *Jehovah, please save us!*

৩৵৯

Daniel thrashed on a straw pallet, his world a haze a pain and despair. A cool hand touched him, placed a cup to his lips. "Drink, my young friend."

He gulped the sour wine, his thirst overpowering his distaste, and opened his eyes. The Babylonian physician, a bald man with kind dark eyes, continued to support him with an arm around his shoulders while he offered Daniel more wine. "You will feel better soon."

Daniel sagged, wanting to lay back down and find escape in sleep. He glanced around the room. Torches set in iron sconces on the wall provided flickering light. Seven other pallets lay on the floor, each with a young man stretched out on it. Someone moaned across from him. Daniel smelled blood and sweat and shuddered.

The physician eased Daniel back on his pallet and stood. With a rustle of his stained white robes he went to check on another young man.

Daniel closed his eyes as tears escaped. The last few days were a nightmare he could only bear to dwell on briefly. He remembered against his will the sight of his father's body, that lay near the chained king's corpse in the throne room, the king's seat itself occupied by Nebuchadnezzar, a short man who glowered at the bodies as if they offended him.

Then there was the forced march to Babylon. He, Mishael, the twins, and other sons of nobles were roped together and forced to walk quickly night and day, with only short breaks for rest. The soldiers barely gave them water and dried goat meat to eat, and Daniel had thought he would die on the way. When they finally reached the Babylonian city of Susa, he began to hope the worst of his ordeal was over.

Then came the surgery.

Daniel could still feel the throbbing pain in his groin. He remembered Rebecca, the beautiful girl his father had point out to him in the market just last month. She had been perusing olives, her dark eyes twinkling when she noticed Daniel staring. When they left the market, his father told Daniel he planned to arrange a marriage between him and Rebecca. "You will have strong sons with her."

Now, there would never be any sons from him. He was the last of his father's house, a house that traced its lineage all the way back to the patriarch Judah. When he died, so would his father's name.

Alone, his dreams for a future shattered, Daniel wept and wondered what more God would permit to be done to him. He cried himself to sleep, and then he dreamed.

He was back in front of Solomon's Temple. There were no Babylonians around this time. Someone had set up two long tables covered in white linen cloth and filled with succulent dishes – lamb simmering in a delicate sauce, fatted calves, tasty quail. Bowls of sparkling red wine sat among the dishes.

Daniel took a step towards the table but a hand on his shoulder stopped him. Someone who resembled a man stood next to him, but Daniel sensed he was no mere man. His skin shone like polished bronze and his robe was so white Daniel could barely look at it. The man's dark eyes blazed but his deep voice was calm as he said, "Wait. Watch."

Daniel turned back towards the tables and saw a number of young Hebrew men had appeared. They fell on the food and wine as if they were starving, quickly consuming the goodies.

As they ate, Daniel noticed a carved stone statue in front of the temple. It also had the appearance of a man. But Daniel had seen likenesses of this horrid mockery of mankind before – the king and many of his neighbors had similar statues. "Baal," he said. "Why is that here, in front of Jehovah's temple?"

"Watch."

Daniel heard a cry of alarm and turned his attention back to the young Hebrew men. To his shock they appeared to be suffering from a wasting disease. Their cheeks had sunk into their faces and their skin clung to their bones. As Daniel stared, a fierce west wind came and the afflicted men shattered into dust.

He wanted to flee that accursed place, but the bright man's hand kept him where he stood. As the wind died down, he noticed things had changed. The abominable statue had vanished. The tables, which had been stained with food and wine from the frenzied feeding of the other men, were clean and filled again. But it wasn't the same kind of food.

Daniel felt the man remove his hand and he approached the table. Now, colorful vegetables filled it– leeks, cucumbers, and zucchini were three he noticed immediately. Stone flagons of water stood next to stone cups.

As he observed the table and wondered what this all meant, a light from above shone down upon it. A voice that sounded like thunder came from the light. "He who honors Me, I will honor."

With a gasp Daniel shot up from his pallet. He was still in the infirmary in Babylon. The physician sat at a table in the corner of the room, apparently reading a scroll by candlelight. He looked towards Daniel. "Are you all right, Belteshazzar?"

It took Daniel a moment to remember that that was his new name – a name bestowed on him by some Babylonian official when he'd arrived in Susa. He shuddered. Something else they tried to take from him – his very name.

The physician rose and came to Daniel, crouching next to him. "Are you in pain? Do you need a sleeping draught?"

The thought of the sour wine made his mouth twist. "No, I'm fine. Thank you."

The physician stared at him a minute, then nodded. "Tomorrow, you and the others will be well enough to begin your education. You will see, things are better for you here." With a pat on Daniel's shoulder he straightened up and returned to his scroll.

Daniel lay back down, his mind whirling. He understood that what he'd experienced was no mere dream. But what did it mean?

⚜

The next day, at the middle of the day, Daniel shuffled into the dining area with some of the other Hebrew youth. Breakfast had been a cup of milk that morning and he was starving.

He looked around the large room. A huge stone fireplace stood unlit at the far end. Long wooden tables with benches marched in two rows on the packed dirt floor. Windows on either side of the room let in bright sunshine.

"Daniel!"

He turned and was relieved to see Mishael waving at him from a nearby table. He gratefully hurried over and eased himself onto the bench, not able to withhold a wince. "Are you all right?"

Mishael frowned. "We are alive, if that counts for anything." Daniel noticed the twins sitting across from him, both with the same pinched expressions. Daniel didn't have to ask why they looked like that – he was sure his face was the same.

Someone jostled him to his right, and he turned to see someone else he knew from Jerusalem. Joses was a tall, thin boy who tended to look down on anyone who didn't meet his social standards. Because Daniel's family clung to the old ways, he looked down on him, too.

Daniel wasn't fond of Joses. But perhaps the time was past for such things. "Joses, it is good to see you are alive."

Joses snorted. "I see somehow you survived as well. No thanks to Jehovah."

Daniel shook his head. "You shouldn't say such things. We left Jehovah, He didn't leave us."

"If Jehovah is so great, then why are we here? Why is your father dead?" Joses asked. He shook his head. "My father says Jehovah isn't as powerful as we thought He was."

Before Daniel could respond, a voice from the front of the room called for silence. Turning away from Joses, he gave his attention to the portly man dressed in yellow robes who stood in front of the fireplace.

The man clapped his pudgy hands together and called out, "We welcome all of you to King Nebuchadnezzar's service. For the next three years, you will be trained in our history, our ways, and our language. And, to demonstrate how important you are to us, you will be fed food and wine from the king's table."

He clapped his hands again. Two men in white robes and turbans entered from the rear of the room, carrying something between them. Daniel blinked when he saw what it was. The statue that was carried on a board the two men held – it looked exactly like the one in his dream!

Two other men followed the first two. One bore a platter of cooked meat; the other a bowlful of wine. Daniel felt himself tense, though he didn't fully understand what was going on. He watched the first pair of men carry the statue to the front of the room and turn so that its leering face was visible.

The fat man who seemed to be in charge bowed to the statue. "The great god Bel, who has given us many victories, please accept this offering from your servants." The official then stepped back and gestured to the men carrying the food and wine.

These two men stepped forward. The one with the platter tipped it over so that the roasted meat fell onto the dirt floor in front of the idol. The second man then poured the wine over the meat. Both of them bowed low to the idol before turning and hurrying out of the room.

Smiling, the official waved at the room. "And now, eat. Drink. Be merry."

Young boys filed into the room, bearing platters of meat and bowls of wine. Others set empty wooden plates and cups before Daniel and the other captives. A server slid a platter of roasted calf meat in front of Daniel, and next to it, a bowl of wine. The sound of chatter, and of wine being poured, filled the room.

Feeling nauseous, Daniel could only stare at the idol in the front of the room. But when Joses reached for the meat, it brought Daniel out of his thoughts. "We can't eat that!" he snapped.

He realized he'd raised his voice when his table fell silent. Joses glared at him. "And why can't we? I'm hungry."

Daniel's stomach growled. He cast a pleading look at the twins and Mishael. "It's been offered to an idol. If we eat it, we defile ourselves before God."

One of the twins had been reaching for a bowl of wine when Daniel spoke. He pulled his hand back, color flooding his olive cheeks. "The wine too?" he asked.

"The wine too." Daniel hated making his friend feel bad but they had to realize the truth of the matter. "Things like this caused Jehovah to turn away from us. The prophet Jeremiah said —"

"That madman?" Joses scoffed. "Who cares what he said? Give me the food if you're not going to eat it."

"But we mustn't," Daniel said. He grabbed the platter as Joses began to pull it towards his plate. "Joses, please listen."

With a yank, Joses got control of the platter. "You need to face facts, Daniel. We're not in Judah anymore. Better to do what they want of us." He used a fork on the platter to spear a piece of meat and transfer it to his plate.

"But Joses..." Daniel began.

"What is going on here?"

Daniel looked at the end of the table. The fat official was standing there, glaring at him. Next to him a brown haired man who didn't look much older than Daniel and his friends shifted his weight from foot to foot.

Daniel wanted to crawl under the table. But he remembered his dream. "Please sir, we cannot eat this food. It would defile us. Please, can't we have something else?"

The man's round face softened. But his tone was firm. "Young man, I can't do as you ask. If the king saw that you were malnourished compared to your peers, he would blame me for it. While I admire your devotion to your God, you must eat what you've been given."

"Please, we can't," Daniel begged.

The official shook his head. "You have no choice." He looked down the table. "Does anyone else wish to refuse to eat?"

Mishael leaned forward. "I agree with Daniel. It is wrong."

The twins bobbed their heads in agreement. Azariah spoke for both of them. "It is wrong."

Daniel was grateful for his friends' support. He noticed that not one other Judean joined with them. Joses ignored it all, shoveling food into his mouth.

The official shook his head. "You four are going to be trouble." Turning to the nervous young man next to him, he said, "Melzar, guard the four of them. Make sure they do what they need to do."

"Yes sir," Melzar said. He walked to where Daniel and the others sat. "I'll take care of it."

"See that you do," the fat man said. With that, he turned and headed to another table.

Melzar cleared his throat. "You must eat," he told them. "What harm could it do?"

Daniel remembered his dream. He glanced at the others, and made a decision. "Would you be willing to test the four of us?"

A line appeared between Melzar's eyes. "Test you?"

"Yes," Daniel said, speaking quickly. "Give us nothing but vegetables to eat and water to drink for ten days. After that, see how we are compared to the others. When you do, make your decision based on that."

Melzar scratched his head. "Ten days...that's all? And you just want vegetables and water?"

"Yes," Daniel said. He glanced at his friends. Mishael looked troubled but nodded his agreement. Hananiah gave a last longing glance at the wine before he sighed and said, "Yes." Azariah echoed his brother's statement.

Melzar shrugged. "Ten days...all right. But no complaining. And if you look worse than the others I'll make you eat the king's food if I have to shove it into your mouth. Understand?"

"Yes," Daniel said. "Thank you."

Melzar sighed. "Don't thank me yet. Wait here and I will get what you asked for." He glanced over where the fat official was laughing with the young men at another table. "If he asks, I'll explain our arrangement. I'm taking a chance on you all; you'd better be right."

After Melzar left Joses sneered, "You are crazy! No meat or wine? You'll be sick before the ten days are over."

"We'll see about that," Daniel said. He turned to his friends. "Thank you for siding with me. I had a dream I think relates to this – we're doing the right thing."

"A dream?" Joses laughed. "Next you'll be calling yourself a prophet." A few of the other Judeans joined Joses in laughter.

Daniel felt his face grow warm. "I'll tell you about the dream later," he told his friends. Doing his best to ignore Joses and the others, he prayed, *God, please let me understand Your will and the dream you sent me.*

෴

T he ten days went by far more slowly than Daniel wished. He spent his days in Chaldean classrooms, going through their education program. Gradually the pain in his groin subsided and he could almost forget what was done to him.

Mealtimes were not easy. The king's food smelled wonderful, especially in comparison to the vegetables Melzar brought them day by day. Joses made a great show of eating his portion of meat, getting others to mock Daniel and his friends for refusing such delicacies.

One night, when Daniel was tempted to give in, he had the dream again. He made sure to tell Mishael and the twins about it, assured that they were doing the right thing. He wasn't sure he would've stuck it out without the support of the others. Together they put up with the jibes of Joses and those like him. Together they stuck to their decision.

The tenth day dawned. Daniel had trouble concentrating on his lessons that morning. What if Melzar decided that Daniel and the others were worse off for not eating the king's food? Would he force them to comply?

When the time came for the midday meal, Daniel entered the dining area with some concern. Mishael clapped him on the back. "It'll be okay," he told him. "Don't forget your dreams."

The twins walked in ahead of Daniel and Mishael. They stopped so suddenly that Daniel nearly ran into them. Looking forward, he saw the portly official glaring at Melzar. "Ten days? You've been doing this for ten days? You said you would deal with them."

Melzar was pale, and his forehead shone with sweat. "It was a small thing...a test..."

"Bah!" the official spat. "Where are they? Let me see how bad off they are."

"We're right here," Daniel said, stepping past the twins. "Don't blame Melzar. I persuaded him."

The official turned and stared at Daniel. There was a long moment of silence. Other young men were entering the room, casting curious glances at the scene in front of them.

As Joses went by, the official reached out and grabbed him by the arm. "You! Stand next to him," he said, pointing at Daniel.

Joses gave Daniel a dark look before standing next to him. Daniel noticed that the other young man had a yellow undertone to his skin and wondered if he was ill.

"I don't believe it," the official muttered. He turned to Melzar. "This one –" he pointed at Daniel – "has been eating nothing but vegetables for nearly two weeks? What about the one next to him?"

Melzar shrugged. "I think the one next to him has been eating from the king's table. But this one and the three behind him have all eaten nothing but vegetables."

The official shook his head. "Look at them! They are clearly more healthy than this one." He glanced around the room. "In fact, they appear better off than anyone else in here."

Daniel felt as if a stone were lifted from his chest. "Please sir, may we continue to not eat from the king's table? Since you see your servants aren't suffering."

The official stroked his round chin. "Very well. Melzar, you are to see to it. Give them nothing but vegetables to eat and water to drink."

"Yes, my lord," Melzar said with a bow.

"What about me?" Joses asked. "Will the rest of us have to eat what they eat?"

The official seemed to consider it, but shook his head. "Only if you wish to. But the king is intent on sharing his table with you – it would be best if only a few refused it."

"I don't want to refuse it," Joses insisted.

"Very well," the official said, dismissing him with a wave. "And you, what is your name?" he asked, turning to Daniel.

Daniel said, "You have named me Belteshazzar, but my name is Daniel."

The official raised an eyebrow, but said, "Very well, Belteshazzar. Learn well our ways...it appears your God is looking out for you. Now go, sit and eat."

Daniel led his friends to their table, remembering the words from the voice that sounded like thunder: *He who honors me, I will honor.*

He didn't know what Jehovah had in store for him here in this strange land. But for the first time since that horrible day he was taken from Jerusalem, he dared to hope that not all his dreams were lost.

Maybe, Jehovah had a plan for him in Babylon. And whatever it was, Daniel would never doubt his God again.

ABOUT "CAUGHT IN ADULTERY"

Our final story is based on an event described in John 8:1-11 concerning a woman caught in adultery brought to Jesus. I'd wondered about her story. The account tells us little. So, fictionally speaking, I decided to fill in the blanks.

CAUGHT IN ADULTERY

E lizabeth shivered as Michael's hand brushed down her side, leaving her skin tingling. She lay back in the bed with its perfumed linen sheets and briefly closed her eyes. Her lover's arrival the night before had been unexpected, but not without its benefits.

An unwelcome memory of her husband Caleb arose. She saw him standing in the main room of their home in Bethsaida, holding out his hands caked with clay from the potter's wheel, tears in his dark eyes as he begged her to stay as she packed bread and dried fruit for her journey.

She hadn't listened. She was tired of being married, tired of Bethsaida. She wanted to go to Jerusalem, start over. She asked Caleb for a divorce, and he refused. So, she left anyway.

A blue and white curtain separated the sleeping area from the rest of the small house she now occupied. A window high above the bed let in air and light. Morning sunlight slanted in, enabling her to see Michael's somber expression when she opened her eyes.

"Love? What is wrong?" she asked, reaching up to caress his bearded cheek.

He started at her touch, then looked down on her with a smile. "I'm sorry, Elizabeth, I have much on my mind."

She pouted. "Do you want to leave?" she asked, letting her fingers run down his bare chest, playing with the hair there.

He groaned. "No, of course not, especially when you do things like that." He bent down and kissed her deeply, and she clutched him, her desire growing.

Suddenly, the curtain was ripped aside. Her gaze went to the opening to the sleeping area, where several men in dark robes stood.

She shrieked, her hands going over her breasts. "Help! Robbers!"

Michael's hand came down over her mouth, muffling her cries. She stared at him, her eyes wide and filled with questions.

"Elizabeth," he said, his voice soft, "I am sorry. Please forgive me."

A man who appeared older than Elizabeth's twenty years with a black hat and white shawl over his head grabbed Michael's arm. "Get dressed and get out. Make sure no one sees you."

"Yes, Rabbi Enos," Michael said, his cheeks bright red.

Enos shook his head. "Go home to your wife. Do not disgrace yourself further."

"M-Michael?" Elizabeth stammered as her lover rose from the bed, not looking at her. She sat up, reaching for him.

The rabbi backhanded her, sending her back on the grass-stuffed mattress. "Be quiet, adulteress. Cover yourself up."

Her hand flew to her cheek, tears spilling from her eyes as she drew the fine woven blanket over her. Between the black-robed men standing in the doorway she saw Michael silently putting on his pants and tunic while one of the strangers appeared to berate him.

"Where are your clothes?" Enos asked, his voice harsh.

She took a good look at him and the other men and suddenly felt cold. *Pharisees.* She looked more closely at Enos and saw how long the fringe of his shawl was. He must be a leader. She avoided the temple, and these men, whom she knew would only look at her with contempt.

"What are you doing here?" she demanded, even as her voice shook.

"We are servants of Jehovah, harlot. We've come to mete out his justice on you."

Her fear grew. "Michael," she called out, her voice pleading. "Michael, stop them, please. Don't leave me with them."

Enos crouched down and grabbed her chin, forcing her to look at him. "Your lover cannot help you. Indeed, he has redeemed himself by giving you to us."

She tried to wrench herself from his painful grasp. "He didn't. He wouldn't."

"Really?" Enos's chuckle was cruel. "We needed to catch someone like you, and Michael was eager to help us with that. Did you not wonder at his appearing last night? At his lingering today?"

She had, but what Enos was saying was too monstrous for her to believe. "Please," she begged, tears spilling from her eyes. "Have mercy."

With a sound of disgust Enos pulled his hand off her face, wiping it on his richly embroidered robe. "There is no mercy for you. Not from us." Looking around the alcove, he snatched up the simple dove-colored dress she'd worn last night. "Get dressed," he ordered, tossing the dress on the bed. Turning his back on her, he spoke to another older man. "Is the Teacher in the Temple yet, Salmon?"

Shaking, she reached for her dress and slipped it over her head as Salmon answered, "He was there earlier – He'd just started teaching. Something ridiculous about a plank in one's eye. I didn't linger."

Elizabeth gazed up at the window. It was small – could she

possibly lever herself up and through it? Maybe if she were quick...

Someone grabbed her arm and dragged her from the bed, letting her fall in a heap on the dirt floor. She cried out in pain and fear, looking up to see the Pharisees glare down at her.

Rabbi Enos turned and spoke to someone over his shoulder. "Aaron and Dan, bring her. We go to the Temple. We'll see Him try to get out of this."

Two younger Pharisees, their faces grim, grabbed Elizabeth by her arms and hauled her to her feet. She fought to free herself, but their grip was hard and painful. They followed the half-dozen men through the darkened main room of her house, the house Michael had given her, Michael, who Enos claimed had betrayed her...

As she struggled, she wondered what was going on. Why were the Pharisees doing this? Who were they taking her to? What was going to happen to her? She knew what the Law said should happen to adulteresses, but they wouldn't dare...would they?

The sunlight momentarily blinded her as they stepped outside. When her vision cleared, she could see her neighbors staring at her, their eyes wide. Some looked fearful, holding their children close to their sides as the group passed. Others frowned at her, as if they thought she deserved her fate.

No one came forward and spoke for her. No one gave her any assistance, or even a glance of pity.

Elizabeth couldn't blame them. Michael had given her the house not long after she caught his eye in the marketplace, where she'd gone to beg for some food. He had kindly bought her roasted grain and a fig cake and talked pleasantly with her. A woman alone had few options, and becoming his lover seemed a good idea at the time.

The neighbors didn't know her very well. And she was certain they whispered about her relationship with Michael.

More fearful than she'd ever been in her life, Elizabeth stumbled along, half-dragged by her Pharisee captors. As they wound through the narrow streets, she did something she hadn't done since she was fifteen and orphaned.

She prayed.

⚜

The golden gleam of the Temple was a thing of beauty and pride to those who lived in Jerusalem. Normally, Elizabeth shared those feelings, even if she avoided the place.

Now, as they got closer, she felt dread pool in her stomach. Whatever these fanatics had planned, it would happen in the Temple. They were taking her to Someone there, and Jehovah alone knew what their goal was.

People made way for the group, and they entered the Temple, heading for its courts. The dirty marbled floor was cold against her bare feet. Ahead of them a small crowd stood, and she could hear a man's voice speaking to them.

"Make way, make way," Salmon called out, and the crowd parted. The men brought Elizabeth forward, in front of a Man sitting on a cedar bench. He wore a blue woven tunic under a white robe stained with dust, and he regarded the intrusion calmly.

Three other men who stood nearby weren't as placid. One of them, with a brown curly beard and muscled arms, spoke up. "Lord..."

The Man held his hand up. "It's all right, Peter. You all go join the others. I will come to you shortly."

With a fierce look at the Pharisees, Peter and the others walked away. The Man turned his attention to the mob before him. "Yes?"

Rabbi Enos lifted his chin. "Jesus, we come with a question for you."

Elizabeth stared at the sitting man. This was Jesus? She'd

heard of Him – it was hard to live in Bethsaida or Jerusalem and not know the name. People said many conflicting things about Him. Some claimed He was a great prophet; others said He was a trickster. Still others repeated tales of sick being healed and the blind given sight.

She wondered why the Pharisees had brought her to Him. She'd heard there was no love lost between them. What was this about?

Enos turned and gestured at her, his voice dripping with contempt. "Teacher, we caught this woman in the very act of adultery. Now, according to the law Moses gave us, such women should be stoned. What say You?"

If the two young Pharisees hadn't held up Elizabeth, she would have fallen to the ground. Stoned? They intended to stone her?

She'd seen the pit outside of Jerusalem, filled with sharp rocks, where stonings took place. Stones of various sizes littered the area. According to what she'd heard, the condemned one would be shoved into the pit, and large stones would be dropped on them until they were dead. The lucky ones died in the initial fall. Others, not so much.

Elizabeth cast a pleading look at Jesus. Would He tell them to stone her? Wouldn't that get him in trouble with the Romans? They controlled Jerusalem – surely, they wouldn't permit this.

Jesus's gaze swept the crowd. He stared at her a moment, and she saw compassion and sorrow in His eyes.

Rabbi Enos stood there, a smug look on his face. Elizabeth realized what was going on, why he'd brought her here. They cared nothing for her – they were trying to lure Jesus into a trap.

If He said to stone her, they could report his statement to the Romans, and they would act against Him. If He said to spare her, he would be speaking against the Law of Moses, and the Pharisees could brand Him a false teacher.

She trembled in fear for herself. Either way, she was certain they intended to put her to death. There was no hope for her. She was paying the price for her sins, and she felt tears stream down her face at the thought of dying.

Jesus stared at Enos, His gaze thoughtful. Then He slid off the bench and stooping to the ground, began to write in the dirt with His finger.

Elizabeth blinked. This was not what she expected. A glance at Enos revealed he hadn't expected it either. The Pharisee looked puzzled, then annoyed.

"Teacher?" he asked. "What should we do with her?"

Jesus said nothing as he continued to write. Elizabeth tried to make out the words, but it was hard to read upside down. She thought she saw Enos's name, and maybe others.

Rabbi Enos took a step forward, nearly stepping on the words in the dirt. "Teacher, I demand you answer us. What say you?"

Slowly, Jesus looked up at Enos. He got to his feet, and the rabbi stepped back. For a moment, silence ruled as Jesus surveyed the group. Elizabeth saw anger flash in his eyes.

Then he addressed them all. "Let he among you without sin cast the first stone."

He stooped back down and began writing again. Elizabeth wanted to plead with Him to help her, save her from these Pharisees. She looked at Enos, expecting him to order her taken to the pit.

Instead, the rabbi was looking at Jesus with...was that dismay? He stared at Jesus with his mouth partially open, his fists clenched.

One of the other Pharisees tugged Enos's arm. "What do we do?"

Enos snapped his mouth shut. He gave her a glare that made her shrink back a step. Then, without a word, he turned and pushed his way through the crowd, leaving the Temple.

Two other Pharisees followed him. The others looked at each

other, shifting their weight from foot to foot. The two young men who held her let go of her arms and stepped back.

One by one, the Pharisees left. Some cast dark looks at Jesus as they left. A couple appeared embarrassed. The two that had dragged her to the Temple were the last to leave, and then they were all gone.

She couldn't believe it. She rubbed her arms, wincing where they'd restrained her. She held her breath, waiting for them to return, to finish what they started.

"Woman, where are your accusers?"

She whirled around to see Jesus standing in front of her. He smiled slightly as He raised an inquiring eyebrow. "Has no one condemned you?"

She stared into His dark eyes. There was kindness there. "No one, Lord," she replied, hardly believing she could say those words.

Jesus nodded. "Neither do I condemn you. Go, and from now on, sin no more."

Her cheeks burned with shame, even as relief coursed through her. He knew of her sin. She swallowed. "Yes, Lord, I will."

His gaze seemed to pierce her soul. "Go home to Caleb, daughter. He is waiting for you."

She trembled. How did He know about Caleb? Surely this was a prophet, as people said. She managed to nod before turning and nearly running out of the Temple, his words running through her mind.

※

"Love?"

Elizabeth turned to see Michael standing in the doorway of the house. She frowned, remembering his behavior that morning and Enos's words. "What do you want?"

Michael stepped inside, shutting the door behind him. "I was worried about you."

She kept a square table between the two of them. Her bag, with her few belongings and some food for her journey, sat on the floor next to her.

"If you were so concerned, why did you leave me with them?" she asked her voice shaking as she fought not to scream the words at him..

He looked stunned. "I had no choice, Elizabeth. They would have accused me if I hadn't obeyed them. You know that."

"They planned to kill me," she told him. "Did you know *that?*"

A brief hesitation, then he stammered, "Of course not. What kind of a person do you think I am?"

She closed her eyes a moment. Enos had told the truth. "You wanted to save your own skin," she said, her voice bitter. "You really don't care about me, do you?"

He started to come around the table, but she held up a hand. "No. Michael...this is wrong. I see that now. We shouldn't be together."

He frowned. "Elizabeth, please. You're upset, I understand that. But I *do* care about you. Let me show you."

She shook her head. "No. I'm going back to Bethsaida. If Jehovah is kind, Caleb will forgive me."

"Go back?" He narrowed his eyes. "You are joking, aren't you?"

She picked up the bag she'd packed and slung it over her shoulder. "No. I was given a blessing today by a prophet from God. He told me to return home and sin no more. That's what I'm going to do."

"A prophet?" he asked, confused.

"Jesus," she said. "I'm sure you've heard of him."

He rolled his eyes. "The Man is a madman. My father-in-law says He's a Sabbath breaker and a deceiver. You can't trust Him."

"It is thanks to Him I am not dead," she shot back. "And He

appears more godly than those who tried to trap Him at my expense. Including you."

"You'll regret this," Michael said. "You'll come back. You'll see."

Elizabeth walked to the door. "No, I won't. Go back to your wife, Michael. That's where you belong."

He stood by the table, a stubborn look on his face. "I won't take you back if you walk out that door."

She shrugged, her anger becoming pity. "So be it. Goodbye, Michael." Opening the door, she stepped out into the afternoon sunlight. For a moment, she lifted her face to the sun, thinking how blessed she was that she was still alive.

Turning, she saw Michael hadn't moved. He stood with his arms crossed, glaring at her.

She shut the door firmly. Then she turned, her gaze sweeping the dusty street, a place that had been where she lived but never home.

She gave a small smile. Jesus had said Caleb was waiting for her.

It was time to go home.

ABOUT THE AUTHOR

Laura Ware's column, "Laura's Look," appears weekly in the Highlands News-Sun and covers news items or ideas she can talk about for 600 words. She is the author of a number of short stories and several novels. Active in her congregation, she teaches a Ladies Bible Class on Tuesday mornings. Her essay, "Touched by an Angel," appeared in *Chicken Soup for the Soul: Random Acts of Kindness*. Laura lives in Central Florida. Check out her website and sign up for her newsletter at www.laurahware.com.

ALSO BY LAURA WARE

Dead Hypocrites

The Silent Witness

Redemption

Seek and Ye Shall Find

Two Weeks in Guyana

www.ingramcontent.com/pod-product-compliance
Lightning Source LLC
Chambersburg PA
CBHW022045170626
46808CB00003B/1369